Shadows Sing vol.1

Shadows Sing vol.1

vol.1

Alyson M. Wilson

Alyson M. Wilson

CONTENTS

I would like to thank Morgan Boyer, for being so kind as to volunteer to be a test readers for this book.

I would also like to thank my family for their encouragement and support during this process.

I want to send a special thank you to my fiends who have chosen to follow this book's side-stories on my blog. I hope that you all have enjoyed reading some lore about this world and have had a some fun while waiting for this book's official release.

Lastly, I want to thank you the reader!
Thank you for taking time to consider reading this book.

Birthday Surprise

Thank God! Today is finally the first day I can live without my Aunt Madeline and Uncle Ernest constantly looking over my shoulder. I know they mean well by worrying and wanting what's best for me, but I have to say this overprotective, planned way of life they live is really starting to get to me. It's so suffocating having to explain where I go and plan to do with my friends. I feel like a prisoner between school and home. Not much room in between to have a social life or experience the world around me.

Well, I guess I should explain. After all, it's not like you know the story. My name is Voxy Ann Rosewell. Voxy Anne is a nickname for my legal name Roxanne. A boy in the sixth grade called me a fox while I was hanging out with my friends and the nickname was a play on the moment. I don't mind, as long as they never call me a fox again. As of today, October 31, I am officially 18 years old. During this summer, I finished my high school education. My Aunt Madeline and Uncle Ernest wanted me to continue my education immediately by taking some college-level classes from home, but I declined. That's the thing about my aunt and uncle; they value education, science, and success more than life and creativity. I've lived with them for several years, though not my entire life.

I did spend eleven months with a foster family before I lived with them. I remember fragments of a painful time with them. However, compared to most people I know who have been in the system, my experience was practically a dream. I think I was around four years old at the time. The family had a sweet dog named Princess, who was fond of me. The foster mother, from my perspective, was a witch who played mind games. Somehow, she made me think it was my fault whenever something unfortunate happened. One example of this was when the dog managed to escape the backyard, and the escape became my fault. The reality was that Princess dug in the backyard for weeks and finally made a big enough hole to escape. Despite her first escape, they never did fill that hole. It happened a lot, and I got blamed a lot. But that was only one of many examples of the twisted mind games she played. The worst was when, out of the blue, she would tell me that it was my fault that my mother had died. I was truly thankful Aunt Madeline and Uncle Ernest collected me after the social worker notified them of my mother's death. That part of my life feels like a hole. As for my father and what happened to him, that's also been a hole.

My aunt and uncle are strict, and it may have to do with my mother's death and my father's absence. I learned she was very creative from glimpses of stories my aunt was willing to share about my mother. Passionate about music and theater. She dreamed of becoming a grand opera star on the stage. When I asked my aunt about my father, neither she nor my uncle knew anything about him. Or they just didn't mention it. Given how intentional they are about keeping things in order and present, it's hard to tell. As a child, I was content with that order. Yet, I have become more resentful and rebellious after hearing my friends talk about playing games, singing songs on the radio, seeing concerts, and favorite TV shows.

In high school, my friends planned outings with me to go to art shows, watch movies, and perform. Sadly, more than half of our attempts have derailed due to my aunt and uncle's misfortune connections with people. One time, my friend Sasha and I decided to go to the art museum one summer with her family. Knowing that my aunt and uncle would refuse, I told them I would spend the day with Sasha and her family without any more details. They assumed that I would just go to her house and play. Neither Sasha nor I knew that a relative of my aunt's coworker had mentioned to my aunt's coworker about the adorable family that came to the museum that day. Sasha and I were mischievous, wandering from hallway to hallway to look at as many pictures as we could in the shortest amount of time. The coworker told my aunt, and I was grounded.

She acknowledged that she should've followed up by making sure that she and my uncle call my friend's parents from then on to be aware of any surprising trips. Sasha also got in trouble with her parents for telling them my family had given me permission to go with them that day when I didn't. It's only been since this summer that they've loosened up on the rules. They remind themselves in conversations that I am becoming an adult this year. It's my responsibility to manage my own life. However, they give me hour-long lectures before I go anywhere. I must stay in groups with friends or just with people when we go out. To always stay in well-lit rooms and park our cars and well-lit parking spaces. I should not eat any food or drink any drink that I didn't order. I shouldn't accept anything that a stranger offers. It feels like the basic rules, but what's basic? I've learned from my friends' families that basic knowledge can vary.

So, they accepted my response when I declined to go to college and live at home with them. However, they're concerned for my future. They remind me that they want what's best for me. A week before my birthday, Uncle Ernest mentioned a job opening for which I should be qualified. 'It offers good benefits for higher education' was the sales pitch takeaway from this conversation. I told him that we would talk more about it after my birthday. I was more concerned about having a special evening with my friends to celebrate becoming an adult. I told him I would figure things out after the celebration. Right now, I just want to spend time enjoying being with them and not worry about being a student or an employee for a while.

As for today, my friends and I planned a great night. We are going to a casino to gamble a little. Then we're going to the movies to catch the latest horror movie, "Wood Dweller." Before we finish the night off, we are going to a club to ring in the midnight hour of my first day being legally an adult. I am super excited. Aside from the movie theater, I've never been to a club or casino.

I would tell you how this birthday started, but it was like any other day with my aunt and uncle. I woke up and got myself ready for the morning. I combed my hair, brushed my teeth, and ate cardboard cereal. I put on my not-so-much casual clothes, which looked more like a fast-food uniform without the business logos or badges. I put my party outfit in my gray tote. Both my aunt and uncle go to work early. I would spend a few hours reading my uncle's science magazines and journals until they got home.

If you haven't guessed yet, my uncle is a scientist. His specialty is in Physics, which plays with light. He told me that he was always fascinated by illusions that lights can create as a child. My aunt is also a scientist. Her specialty is in Medicinal Chemistry. Since the rise of home remedy social media videos, her work has focused on testing the myths and providing scientific explanations for why some work. Most are scams for quick cash grabs. My aunt would then have to help create a plan to help hospitals navigate the false information and explain the potential harm those scams create. My aunt would get home before my uncle, usually close to noon. She often says her work is never done when coming home and making meals for the family. She always encourages me to help her cook. She reasoned that I could understand how chemicals in specific foods interact. I should know what makes a meal healthy and beneficial to eat. Although I appreciate her enthusiasm to be a teacher in science, I mostly enjoyed helping her cook because it was more of a creative outlet for me.

After helping my aunt make lunch for us, we talked about her day at work, and I talked about the articles that I've read in the magazines left in the house. Then we would listen to the news for a while before it was time for my friends to come and pick me up for the party. My aunt hugged me and told me to be safe when we heard my friend Damien's car horn beep outside. When we got out, my uncle's car turned onto our street. He only had enough time to see me off. He parked his vehicle behind Damien's, turned off the engine, and came out of the car to give me a quick lecture. Surprisingly, Damien also got a quick lecture about not parking closer to the sidewalk. Damien checked the car. My aunt scuffed and told my uncle to let it go.

"Damien, your parking is fine," my aunt said to him, "This old man is cranky because a meeting didn't go well."

"How would you know?" my uncle replied.

"Simple," replied my aunt, "I've lived with you for how many years now. And this isn't the first time a meeting hasn't gone well for you. Whenever a meeting doesn't go well, I have noticed that you become pricklier about details. I also know that you had a meeting today. Therefore, based on your prickly demeanor right now and your schedule. It's only safe to assume that the meeting did not go well if the pattern of behavior stays relevant."

Uncle Ernest went silent.

"There. I was right," my aunt said, "Anyway, be safe and be smart while having fun this evening, everyone. I will take this grouchy man inside and make him a delightful meal to see if we can change this day for him."

Uncle Ernest hugged me and kissed me before heading inside with Aunt Madeline. I got in the car with Damien and the others. As I closed the door, I heard my aunt and uncle whisper to each other. But I couldn't make out what they said. I can only assume my aunt was commenting further on my uncle's demeanor and didn't want to make a fuss about it in front of us.

My friends shared some gossip and played our favorite songs on Penny's phone as we drove off. The evening felt like it flew by so quickly. When we stepped into the casino, I felt like I was in a theme park with all the sounds and lights. I can only recall playing four games. By the time we got to the last quarter, we had less than ten minutes to get to the movie theater. When we got to the movie theater and found our seats, the movie's first five minutes had already passed, but we enjoyed the rest. Penny grabbed Damien anytime the killer did a surprise jump scare on-screen or when we knew that the killer was right behind their next victim. Sasha, at one point, screamed so loud in the theater that no other scream or startling sound could be heard. The people beside us were genuinely concerned for her, and a few theater staff came and checked on her. I didn't know whether to laugh or cry at the situation. This was the first time we'd ever watched a scary movie together. I never knew Sasha was a screamer.

When she heard me chuckle at the situation, she rolled up her popcorn bag and popped me on the head with it. Clearly upset that I thought the situation was funny. After the movie, we went to the club. Damien's cousin, Bruce, worked for this club and scheduled us in advance. It's a hard club to get into if you don't know someone who works there. You can't go spur of the moment. People who attend schedule months if not years in advance just to have a night to hang out there. Bruce started his job with them as a part-timer when he was a senior in high school. He has worked there full-time for close to three years now. He was a part of our little group back in high school, but we don't get to see him as much since he started working there full-time.

Bruce met us when we first set foot into the club. He wanted to spend time with us now that we are getting close to graduating and being graduated. I think this part of our party was his way of saying sorry for not being there for us these past few years.

"Man, if it's not good to see you guys," Bruce's husky voice rang out.

Bruce is wearing a fine black tux with an aqua blue dress shirt. He also had a diamond earring on his right ear. His hair was slicked back and was styled in a way to show his strong jawline.

"Where are the restrooms?" I asked Bruce.

Bruce looked at me and smiled his million-dollar smile. "It's right over there. Down the hall to your right, birthday girl," Bruce replied, pointing to the far-left corner of the room, where there was a hallway.

"So, will you give us a trick or treat?" Bruce teased.

He knew me well enough that I would never wear business casual clothes if I could get away with wearing something much more fun.

"You'll just have to be surprised," I half-heartedly teased back.

"I think I'll go fix up my make-up with you," Sasha said, "Thank you, Damien!"

Sasha sent him a flirtatious look. She took my hand, and we left for the bathrooms.

"Sure thing," we hear Damien say behind us as we force her way through the crowd.

When we got to the bathrooms, I went into the closest stall by the door out of habit. Sasha went to the sink to fix her make-up and started an idle conversation with me. I can't say for sure when, but I think she had a bit of a crush on Bruce when we were freshmen. When we were juniors, she wondered if she should've asked Bruce to go with her to prom. Damien thought she was nuts for not trying. Yet she always talked herself out of it. She'd started thinking he was too busy with work and that his work should be a priority rather than a silly little night out. She knew that we knew it meant something to her that she didn't.

"Did you see the size of that stage in the middle of the room?" Sasha started the conversation, "I wonder if they have concerts here when it's not used as a dance club?"

"Yeah, I did see the stage," I replied, "It looks like it could be used for many things. Live concerts might be one. Maybe they have a DJ come and play on occasions too. It would be fun if they turned it into a karaoke stage."

"That's right. I forgot," Sacha said with a sigh.

"What's the matter?" I asked.

"O'. I just thought it would have been a better evening if we took you to a karaoke bar to sing your heart out instead. We overthought what we wanted to do with you that we didn't consider what you would've enjoyed doing. We know how much you love music, Voxy. You really are an amazing singer. The drama and music teacher through a fit at your aunt for not letting you participate in our high school plays during our first year," Sasha said.

"I think it's more because no one wanted to participate in the performances," I replied.

"That's a load of shit, and you know it," Sasha snapped, "You can out-sing birds, and you know it. Don't believe me; We'll put the matter to rest with the others outside."

"Don't make the others think that this was a miserable night. You know it was a lot of fun, and you deserve to be able to see Bruce again after these years," I replied.

Sasha pretended not to hear me.

I came out of the stall showing off my Gothic attire for the evening. It was a purple velvet top with long flowing sleeves, black lace, and a black bow in the middle. I wore a short black skirt also velvet with gray lace. Long gray and black striped stockings with purple boots with an inch heel. I looked at my reflection in the mirror. I liked these dark-colored clothes because they accented my natural red hair and brown eyes. It was short and an unfortunate bowl shape cut. Sasha knew how to style it to look more like a messy bob. She fixed my hair before we headed out. She had a fantastic gift for styling hair. Sasha had dyed her hair green, but it was originally black. She used to style it in many ways. One day it was in braided ponytails. The next day she had an afro, and the day after that, corn rolls. She was wearing a simple yet elegant black dress. It also complimented her skin tone, which was a golden brown. I think the dress was to impress Bruce and make her look more appealing to him. She is a genuinely strong-willed woman. Yet she is self-conscious when it comes to Bruce. What he thinks and what he likes. We returned to our friends, who were waiting for us at a table that Bruce had reserved.

"It took you long enough," Damien called out to us, "Why do you two always have to spend so much time dolling yourselves up. Even Penny can get dressed quicker than you two."

Penny jabs Damien with her elbow for the comment.

"Ow! What was that for?" Damien asked

"Look how sharp and sassy you look, Voxy!" Penny says.

Bruce chimes in with a whistle and says, "You girls look fine. Can I get anything for you two to drink?"

"Thank you, Bruce. I would like some water," I said.

Bruce looked at me, placed an arm on my shoulder, and said, "You know you're in my house now, right. And if an older man can order you a good drink, you should really take up his offer. It's not like I will tell your aunt and uncle if you had a spirit or two."

"Thank you for your offer. Water would be appreciated, Bruce," I said firmly.

"And what would you like to order, miss?" another masculine voice said behind me and Bruce, who still had his arm on my shoulder.

"A tonic if you have any," Sasha said.

She was as surprised as Bruce, and I was to have an unexpected guest sneak up behind us. It may not have helped that we watched a horror flick before coming.

The man was well-dressed like Bruce. He was two inches shorter than Bruce. His voice was likely tenner if he was to sing. He had a fuller face than Bruce's strong jawline but not completely rounded. His figure was fair, not as athletically built as Bruce's figure. He was wearing a solid white tuxedo with a white dress shirt. The sleaves had silver threaded detailing, and he wore an antique-looking pendant with a red jewel hanging from his white bowtie. He has fair pale-colored skin, whereas Bruce is solid ebony. Yet what was genuinely unsettling about this stranger was his eyes. The color of his eyes stood out to me and caught me off guard. His eyes were pink, and the pupil was red instead of black. It reminded me of the teacher's classroom pet rabbit back in the fourth grade that was albino.

I wondered if it was real or a lens used to change his eyes' color. In middle and high school, I noticed printed lenses that changed an eye's color tend to look boxy. Studying his eyes, it didn't seem to be the case. Was he perhaps albino? When he saw me staring into his eyes, I quickly looked away from his gaze. I focused on the conversation between Bruce and Sasha about her choice of drink.

Apparently, Bruce was giving Sasha a hard time for not considering ordering an alcoholic beverage, too. Sasha seemed to be wavering a little on her decision and willing to drink if Bruce offered to pay. They looked at me as if they were going to ask if I would tell her parents if she did. I told them I had no intention of telling them if she chose to accept Bruce's offer. They seemed relieved, but it felt like a low bar for them to accuse me of such a thing. They should know me by now on the matter of helicopter parents.

Then the stranger told Bruce, "Well, it seems that everyone has ordered. Bruce, you need to get back to work. I am not paying you to spend time socializing with your friends. And by the way, don't call this your house just because you work here."

"Yes, sir," Bruce said as a stranger started to walk away.

As the stranger walked away, I noticed how white his hair was and closely matched his white tax.

"Who is that guy?" Penny asked.

"My boss," Bruce replied, "He is one of the club's owners. He doesn't go by his legal name. He used to give out a fake name to employees until we noticed it wasn't his real name.

He said he didn't use his real name because of family matters when we asked about it. He decided to let his employees call him whatever they wanted as long as it was appropriate. So, we just call him Mr. White."

"How come you've never mentioned your boss to us? If I had known you had a boss who looks like that, I would've never taken in the girls to see a horror movie this evening," Damien said, shocked and embarrassed, "The dude be a creepy man."

"Look, Mr. White might be unsettling at first. But when you've worked here as long as I have, you learn he's an easy-going and dependable guy. It's understandable that he wants his employees to work while on the clock. On that note, I better get your orders filled. He was nice enough to overlook my time catching up with you all. But I want to keep my job," Bruce said to Damien.

Then Bruce left to go to the bar and get our drinks. We felt a little awkward after. Unsure what to say next. Sasha broke the ice after a long silence and asked Damien to take Penny dancing while we waited for drinks. Damien felt even more embarrassed, but Penny was delighted and pleaded for Damien to take her dancing.

Finally, Damien said, "Alright, alright. I'll dance with you till your heart is content if it will make you happy."

The reluctant but smooth operator took his lady dancing while Sasha and I watched from the side. Then Sasha broke the silence again.

"You're right. I shouldn't mention the whole karaoke thing to them. I was looking forward to seeing Bruce again, and I feel guilty about using your party as an excuse to see him," she said.

"I understand, and I'm still having an amazing night with you guys. I'm also glad to be able to see Bruce again and see if you will finally tell him how you feel. Besides, there will always be many more birthdays where we can sing our lungs out," I tried to assure her.

She grins but still seems to feel guilty. She had no intention of telling Bruce about her feelings this evening.

We sat for a few more minutes of silence until Bruce came back with our drinks. A few minutes later, what looked like an expensive cake was brought to our table. It was a two-layered cake with vanilla frosting, and pieces of strawberries were cut into flowers for decoration.

"What is this?!" I said in shock.

Sasha was just as stunned as I was. Damien and Penny returned from dancing and were as surprised as we were about the cake. Bruce didn't seem to care about our reactions. Most likely, this cake was a part of his plan for us to celebrate this evening.

"Bruce, we can't eat all this cake!" Damien blurted.

"Hush," Bruce said, "just consider it the great birthday challenge between you all."

"Really! You're going to leave us with a mountain of cake while you return to work?" Damien asked hotly.

Bruce smiled, gave Damien the cutting knife, waved to us, and returned to work.

"Really, man! You can sometimes be a real piece of work," Damien called out to Bruce.

"Perhaps it's just his way of saying sorry he can't spend more time with us," I told the group.

"Right," Damien said, unconvinced.

"How should we tackle Mt. Candyland?" Penny asked.

"One bite at a time," Damien responded half-heartedly.

He cut the cake and gave us each a small piece to start with. I got the first piece, and Damien said, "Happy Birthday, Voxy!"

Penny and Sasha chimed in after him saying happy birthday. They got their slices of cake next then Damien served himself last. I took a bite of my piece of cake, which was terrific. It seemed like a strawberry shortcake with fresh strawberry pieces inside the yellow cake sheet and chunks of strawberry in the filling frosting. Halfway through eating my piece, something about the cake seemed off and almost repulsed me. It didn't taste as it did with the first bite into it.

The texture tasted more and more like sandpaper, and the frosting began to taste like wax. I couldn't help but make a face of disgust. Before the others noticed, I spat the rest of the cake out of my mouth and into a napkin that came with my glass of water. What's going on? This has never happened before. I wonder whether they taste the same thing too. I looked around, but everyone seemed to be enjoying the cake. I tried again to take another bite, but it tasted just as bad. I can't risk spitting it out again. I ended up quickly swallowing it. It was awful, and I regret it. Far better to spit it out than to force it down.

"How's the cake?" Bruce asked, returning to our table, "Amazing, isn't it? I had it specially ordered from the bakery two blocks down the road. Their croissants are to die for. I knew their cakes would be just as good."

"It's wonderful," Sasha said with a mouth full of cake.

"It's delicious," Penny said. Damien gave a thumbs up of approval while he finished chewing.

"Now, since you only have thirty minutes to ring in the end of your special day, Voxy, how about a quick birthday dance?" Bruce said with his million-dollar smile.

2

A Different View

I suddenly felt Sasha's eyes on me. I felt that she wanted to dance with Bruce before night's end. She is too scared to interject.

"I am pretty full after eating all that cake, but I'm sure Sasha would love a chance to dance before we have to go," I said politely and carefully as I could.

"How about I show you around the club while your friends dance?" a familiar voice said.

It was Mr. White walking to our table. Was Bruce in trouble again, I wondered.

"You can get a good view of the dance floor on the second-floor balcony," Mr. White said to me, "Are you afraid of heights?"

"Not particularly, no," I replied.

"I think we can let your friends dance to their hearts' content, and we'll have a birds' eye view," he said casually.

I quickly looked over to Penny and Damien. Damien seemed to be looking in my direction with concern. Penny clung to Damien at the thought of being able to dance. Sasha didn't mind. Her thoughts were on dancing with Bruce. I didn't know if it was a good idea, but I agreed to go with Mr. White. The five of us got up from our table, and I went with Mr. White to the second-floor balcony.

On our way up the stairs, Mr. White said to me, "You can stop worrying. I have no intention to harm you. Though it is good to know that you have some healthy sense of skepticism. The fact is I'm trying to help you get as far away from Bruce as I can."

"Why are you trying to keep me away from Bruce? We've been friends since high school," I asked.

"And in that year of high school, was he flirtatious and manipulative at times between you and your friend with the green hair?" Mr. White asked.

I went silent.

We had many uncomfortable moments like that request to dance this evening. I told Bruce I was not interested in him when I felt my relationship with Sasha was becoming strained that year. Still, it never changed how he treated Sasha and me. The only thing that did change was that Sasha became aware of how I felt. I wouldn't get in between her and her relationship with Bruce.

"Then I'll assume that the answer is yes," Mr. White said, "You've got a good intuition when it comes to judging people and being able to read the situation presented to you. I could tell when you were firm in your choice to drink water. Honestly, I would've stopped him from taking your order if you agreed to his offer."

"Why? Isn't his job to take my order?" I asked.

"You look like one of my cousins," Mr. White said casually, "I would be disgusted if a character like him did to you, or my actual cousins, what he has done with some of the female customers he likes. Many thankfully have the sense to refuse if they're not interested in him, like you. Those who often like Bruce let him play his game, like your friend with the green hair. Yet I think you and I know that your friend isn't aware that Bruce is not interested in a committed relationship with any woman. He tries to keep one-night stands with his clients."

"Tries?" the word came out of my mouth before I could think.

Mr. White smiles.

"He does, on occasions, see some again if they're interested in repeating that night," Mr. White replied.

When we got to the balcony, the view was amazing. I spotted Penny and Damien dancing away like no one was watching. It was different than when they danced a while ago. They're a bold couple when they think no one is watching them. I chuckle a little at the thought. Mr. White seemed to notice.

"I guess your coupled friends act differently when they think no one is watching," Mr. White said. Then he pointed out Bruce and Sasha to me. Something seems off with Sasha, but Bruce seemed to be his usual self.

"Seems like the alcohol Bruce recommended is doing its job. She's drunk," Mr. White said.

I guess the cake didn't help absorb the alcohol. I then recalled what Mr. White said about his cousins on the way up the stairs.

I begin to ask, "Mr. White? I know it's none of my business, but I heard from Bruce that you don't use your legal name, and it's because of family matters. I could be misunderstanding the situation, but...."

Mr. White cut me off and said, "O' that. There might be some misunderstanding. Indeed, I don't use my legal name with employees. I prefer only my family members to call me by my name. People can call me whatever they want if it isn't anything vulgar. No, I don't have a terrible relationship with my family, and I love them. Still, I confess that some of my family may not entirely love me."

Mr. White grabbed the antique pendant off his bowtie and started passively biting on its jeweled end. I think Mr. White was uncomfortable talking about his family and likely started a bad habit of chewing to deal with the anxiety. After a moment of Mr. White chewing, He started the conversation again, to my surprise.

"My mother told me this morning that I should expect one of my red-haired cousins to pay me a visit at the club today for a conversation," he said.

He paused for a moment before continuing, "When the staff told me that a girl matching her description arrived and Bruce was the one taking her order, I became concerned. I thought it was her, but it turned out to be you and your ...."

"O', so that is why you met with us earlier!" I interrupted.

Mr. White did not seem to mind the interruption.

A few seconds passed, then I asked, "Did you find your cousin?"

"No, not yet. She seems to be running late. That's why I will spend my time here to keep an eye out for her," he said.

"Make sense. You can see a lot from up here," I said.

I looked out to find my friends again but suddenly started to feel dizzy. Nauseated too. Mr. White put a hand on my shoulder and asked me if I was alright.

"The room is spinning," I replied.

"Let's go outside so you can get some fresh air," he said.

As we were heading out, it could have been my perception, but it looked like Mr. White was not doing well either.

"Since you have asked many questions from me this evening, can I ask you a few, Voxy?" Mr. White asked as we were heading outside.

"Sure," I said hesitatingly.

I don't think I told Mr. White my name is Voxy. Perhaps Bruce talked about us to him before. I wanted to ask, but he was right. I had asked a lot of questions already.

"Thank you. I would like to know why your friends call you Voxy? I doubt it's your real name like mine is not Mr. White," he asked.

"O' that," I said, remembering.

I explained what happened in the sixth grade, and he started laughing.

"Voxy Ann. For a playful way to say, Roxanne. I have to give credit for creativity to your friends," he said.

When we got outside, I didn't feel any better. Mr. White could likely tell, and we sat on a step on the staircase at the back door.

"Tell me, if you are able, what do you really think of your friend Bruce after learning that he hooks up with the women he serves alcohol to?" Mr. White asked.

"I can't say that I approve. Don't you have policies to protect your customers from rape?" I asked.

"Aw,' You consider it rape. I wonder when a drunk who has a one-night stand considers themselves a victim of rape if they were too drunk to remember consenting to sex. I can say that we haven't had any complaints about his behavior yet. We've checked on the women he has slept with. Still, he could be tempting luck. Like I said earlier, most women who are not interested don't accept his offer, and those interested in playing his game let him. I think you may be on to something; his luck may be running dry and can cost us lawsuits," Mr. White said, reflecting on the matter.

Mr. White looked at me. I must have looked as bad as I felt. The spinning feeling has not stopped yet. I hear Mr. White talk to me, but I can't hear.

I thought I heard him say, "...running late. And on... blood... Rox... van Kurt."

I try, but words are becoming buzzing sounds now. My vision is losing focus too. The next thing I remember was another shape in black moving around. Sounds higher pitch than Mr. White's buzzing sound. Female perhaps. I see some red shining. I feel fingers prying my mouth open. The red shine is close. Is it in my mouth? Feels like a rock. I feel heat and buzz by my left ear. I think I hear the word bite. Bite what? Bite red? I can't ask, mouth full. My teeth feel funny. Feel... feel. What does this feel like? O, Like when I tried to plug my lamb and had my hand on the metal part. O'!!! It feels like I'm being electrocuted! What's shocking me? How do I stop it? I tried to scream for help, but the feeling stopped as quickly as it had started. I see two faces looking down at me. I'm on the ground. A shiny red jewel larger than Mr. White's was over my head. The jewel kind of looked like a large shark tooth on a silver chain. Did I bite that? Was that jewel shocking me?

"How are you feeling, Roxanne? Do you need any more food?" an unfamiliar voice asked me.

"She'll not understand what you mean by calling what happened food. It's her first time eating like us," I hear Mr. White say.

I take a moment to collect myself. I thought I was in pain from the shock, but I didn't feel any pain. The spinning feeling stopped, my vision was back to focus, and my nausea was gone.

"I think I'm fine," I replied, "Did I bite the tooth-looking thing?"

"Yes, it's a special stone that helps people like us," The unfamiliar voice replied.

I turned to see a person with looked practically identical to me. She had brown eyes and red hair like mine. She was wearing a long black cloak. I felt confused because her voice sounded like a low alto. She could probably sing tenner if she really wanted to.

"People like us?" I ask.

"Yes, you're still you but different now. O' how to best explain it?" This new person said.

"Your dormant vampire blood woke up, Roxanne," Mr. White said bluntly.

I turn my attention back to him, trying to understand what he just said.

"Why would you say that?" The red-haired woman yelled at Mr. White.

"Please, little red prince, shut up," Mr. White said coldly.

The red-haired woman grabbed Mr. White's caller.

"Never call me prince again," She warned.

"Sorry to interrupt this moment," I interjected myself into the conversation, "Is she your cousin you talked about earlier? The one you thought I was back at the club."

The woman seemed to want to say something, but Mr. White spoke first.

"Yes, this is my cousin August. I may have to confess that I was not fully honest with you back in the club. I was only expecting to see her only because I was informed that she was assigned by your father to watch over you when your birthday came this year. My mother knew two years in advance that you would be celebrating with your friends at our club," Mr. White said with a bit of displeasure in his voice.

It did not sound like he cared for his cousin. If he did not tell me earlier that he loves his family and goes out of his way to keep a person like Bruce away from them, I would have thought he hated August. Perhaps he is mad that she was late.

"I don't get it. What is so special about this year?" I ask.

"It's not this year, but every year during this time. I and the others, your half-sisters, look after you in case your blood woke up. It could have happened any year. Historically it only happens around the day of the individual's birth. Your blood could've remained sleeping for many years. The longest sleep recorded for a half breed was seventy-nine years," August said carefully.

"What half-sisters and half-breed?" I repeated, still processing what all this meant.

"Yes," August said, then she stopped.

I quickly glanced over at Mr. White. Mr. White seemed to hint to August not to help me put the pieces together. Okay, so I need to think. Half-sisters who watch over me on my birthday due to my father's request. My mother died when I was young. I don't remember having sisters, and I do not remember my father. I lived with my mom's sister, Aunt Madeline, and her husband, Uncle Ernest. They're human; mom must have been human. I'm half-human. That would mean the other half of my blood they refer to is my dad's blood.

"Okay, so if I am seeing this picture correctly. My mother and her family are human. I guess my dad is a vampire. That would explain the half-breed and vampire blood waking comments. I don't remember having sisters, and Aunt Madeline never mentioned anything about me having other siblings. If I have half-sisters, I would guess you're my dad's children. So does that mean that...?" I got interrupted by Mr. White.

"You're on the right track, and I will save you a step. August is my cousin biologically. But you are not biologically my cousin. However, I'll likely call you my cousin in the future since you will be a member of your father's family. As for now, I have to get back to work. I'll let your friends know that you were not feeling well and that I called a taxi to take you home when they are sober," Mr. White said dismissively.

"So do I get to call you by your actual name instead of Mr. White since we're cousins?" I asked.

I did not really care if he did or did not tell me. I've got used to calling him Mr. White.

Mr. White paused and said, "There is no harm in sharing. But I'll tell you the next time we meet if you still have not figured out my name before then. Until then, cousins."

At first glance, we did look similar for half-sisters. I couldn't notice right away if we had any differences in our appearance because of our mothers. I suppose the red hair we got from our father. I know my mother had brown eyes. I guess our father had brown eyes too. If Mr. White is related to August, her mother could've had red albino eyes, like Mr. White. Well, at least a gene for it.

"August, are you a full-blooded vampire then?" I asked.

"I am. I should mention that there are three different types of vampires depending on two traits. The first trait is how we consume living energy, and the second trait is how we grow our types' population. Let's get walking, and I'll explain on the way," August said.

We started walking, although I did not know where we were going. August was so keen to help educate me I didn't have the heart to interrupt and ask.

August started by saying, "Two types of vampire population grow the same way through reproduction and one type that cannot reproduce. Instead, they infect those they feed on, becoming that type of vampire. You likely heard of this type of vampire in horror stories. A vampire bites their prey, drinks their blood, and then that prey becomes a vampire too. The prey often becomes a puppet under the control of the one who originally bit them. We call this type the infected. At best, those infected can only live a hundred years from when they were bitten. Their population has dwindled over time, but it casts a long dark shadow on the other two types of vampires who don't infect and can live in harmony with creation. Kalt Van Schlager, I and you are members of these two types of vampires. I'm sorry Kalt didn't just tell you his name, like a normal person. He likes to play games with people to hold some sort of power over them. But I am not ashamed to tell you his name so he can't play games with my family. I'll not let him treat you as being inferior because you're a half-breed. By being albino, he is considered by all three types as pure-blooded, or highest standing vampire by birth."

"So, what are the two types, and how do we fit into them? I saw Mr. Whi... K...Kal..t... Well, you know who I am talking about. I saw him biting on a red jewel pendant before I got sick. Then, when I came around, I saw that red jewel shark tooth you had close to my face. You both also talked about feeding during that time. Do we eat jewels?" I asked.

August laughed.

"No, we don't eat jewels. We use these stones for emergency food storage. You are probably wondering why you had to wait for me and not simply bite Kalt's pendent and not get that sick. There is the problem of types. As you call them, our jewels are not the same even if they look the same. Kalt consumes blood, and his type is simply referred to as blood eaters. He does not turn people into vampires when he feeds. The pendant's jewel is a unique bloodstone. It takes in spilled blood and stores it for later feedings when he can't hunt for blood. Even if he were to feed on a sheep's blood, most humans would think of him the same way you likely thought of us. That he was an infected vampire. With that being said, infected vampires have their own bloodstones to manage their population. It helps provide them the right to feed and exist as much as any other type of vampire. However, because they both consume blood, Kalt's type of kin has been wrongly persecuted for an infected feeding. Humans and, for a time, vampires couldn't understand the differences between types," August explained.

She took a moment to breathe.

August continues with, "We should count ourselves lucky then, Roxanne. Our type is so different; some vampires don't want to consider us their kin. We eat the same core meal but only by different means than blood. We consume living energy through sound waves. We surprise and scare humans to feed on their energy. If you knew what type of vampire you were when your blood woke and how to feed on sound, in theory, you could have consumed the living energy of those socializing in the club. Since you're still learning to eat our way, you will likely be sharing food from my amulet until you grasp what eating raw sound waves energy is supposed to feel like. Or until you get an amulet with a sound stone of your own. That is what my red tooth-shaped jewel is, a sound stone. It would have been a nightmare for you if you did try to consume blood as a sound eater. Our bodies can't naturally break apart blood and take in life energy that way. We eat life energy directly through our own energy like a net or a spider's web but only in areas of high life activity that produce lots of life energy. And our amulets work the same way. They take in sound waves and concentrate the life energy inside the stone. We then bite the stone to concentrate the flow of collected energy into our energy."

"So, we are like a rechargeable battery that needs a power outlet to feed us energy," I say.

"We are more flexible than a need for a power outlet. Our food is everywhere, but some places are preferable to others. Even sound-eating vampires can still thrive in rural lands or barren deserts," August explained.

"Now that I think about it. I did think before I started feeling better than I was being electrocuted. I can only assume that that was not electricity but the pure living energy you described in your sound stone," I said reflectively.

August looked sheepishly at her feet.

"I'm sorry it felt that way to you. I can imagine if you don't know what is happening or supposed to happen, it can be a frightening experience," She said.

"Honestly, even if you did try to explain to me what was happening back then, I would've had a hard time believing you. That biting a rock would help me feel better from being that sick. So don't worry about showing up late," I replied, trying to assure her.

"I guess that's true. But if that's the case, why did you accept that your vampire blood woke?" August asked.

"Well, I can't fully say that I accept the idea that I am a vampire. I understand that you dealt with my sickness with your amulet. I probably wouldn't if I hadn't seen Mr. White bite his and mention that it's how your type feed. Weirdly without explaining anything about vampires to me, he presented clues to make what was happening understandable. Heck, I still don't know if I believe we're related. Yet you and him seemed convinced that I am. I take it that you and he are not that close," I replied.

"First off, let me help you work on his name so you can start calling him by it. It will not look good for you if you can't call a person by their name. By relying on a nickname, it sounds like you don't care to know who you're talking to or referring to. Our sisters, I, and the rest of our clan will never call you Voxy. We'll only ever call you Roxanne or Roxanne Van Kurt.

My name is August Van Kurt, and our deviant cousin is Kalt Van Schlager. His name and his family name are German. They've been descendants of a vampire line that originated in Germany. And much like his name means, he is a cold-hearted bat. So, his name is Kalt. From now on, I want to hear you call him Kalt when you are talking about him," August said as her temper on the subject seemed to be flaring.

"Alright, I'll call him Kalt. But I'll need to practice. I don't really know any German," I say, feeling embarrassed, "Thank you for looking after me, August."

"I hate him because he insists on misidentifying my gender and knows that I take it personally when he does," August said.

A moment of silent pass, mostly because I did not know how to respond. I recall August grabbing Kalt's caller because he called her a prince. I don't think bringing that memory up in conversation would help matters now.

"I know you don't know why I'm sensitive about words and using proper names. After all, you and I never had a chance to grow up together. I was at birth considered biologically male and the only male born in our family. For us vampires, the majority who govern in the council of clans are males born to each clan's leader. Our father is a clan leader. I was, since birth, expected to fill that role of a successor. There are very few exceptions for why a female would ever be a member of that governing body. Suppose a clan leader doesn't have a male child to govern. In that case, the clan presents a competent daughter that the father and council raise to make thoughtful decisions. To help ensure that no type of vampire ever has more power than the rest and ensure no taboos within our culture are ever broken. Kalt's mother is a member because the council raised her, and her father picked her among his two daughters. When I came out as a trans female, it couldn't be simply a family matter between my father and sisters. It was a matter to be taken to the council. I had to come out to everyone who ruled how I understood myself and why I identified as a female rather than a male. Kalt and his mother were there. Despite the council's approval to let me continue as my father's successor as a daughter rather than a son, I have more eyes watching me from the council. Kalt will never let me forget that I have been a participant as a male and refuses to acknowledge me as a female for these past years," August shared.

She started to cry.

I can't imagine how uncomfortable she must have felt for coming out that way. She does have a good reason to be angry with Kalt. It still doesn't make sense to me why he would do that. Kalt was cold to August, sure. But nothing at least seemed to me that he particularly hated her. Of course, I have learned this evening that I might not be able to scratch the surface when it comes to really knowing who people are, even when I think I know someone. I think Sasha will have a moment of joy being with Bruce only to discover how he saw her and me as nothing more than a game, not even friends. It could be the same lace of knowing a person regarding my perception of Kalt. I raised my left hand and put it on August's shoulder. She looked over at me.

"You're an amazing person, and I am glad to have a sister like you," I said. After some space of sobs, sniffles, and hugs, I managed to ask the main question that had been on my mind since we left the club.

"So, where is it that we are going?" I asked.

"We are almost home. It makes sense for us to live with our father until we're married or I officially become our clan's head. Our family stays together. The reason we couldn't collect you sooner was that you had a right to live as a human until your blood woke. I expect our father will want to speak with you before you rest. Your sense of time will feel different and off for a few days. You also haven't had a lot to eat. I'll need to go hunting after I drop you off. My sound stone did not collect a lot, and I ate most of the energy I had before I found you," August said.

"I understand. Do I need to address our father by name?" I asked.

I felt unsure how I could even begin to start a conversation with a person who had never been a part of my life. The customs of this culture have me concerned about how easy it is to say or do the wrong thing.

"Only if he asks you to call him by his name. Father isn't that formal with us, but we are still expected to show respect to one another and him. Let him start the conversation if you're uncomfortable with speaking to him. After you see the kind of person he is, I am sure that having a conversation with him will become easier. It looks like we are here," August said empathetically.

I had not noticed how far we must have walked. I was so invested in the conversation I wasn't aware of my surroundings. The place around us looked utterly unfamiliar to me. I would say that the club was within reasonable walking distance, but the feeling in my legs suggests otherwise. Just how far did we walk? The club was in the city's heart, but this looked like we just have been walking through the woods. I think this wooded area could be a park, but most of the parks near my aunt and uncle never had this many trees. I wonder if this is the other side of the city. But how did we get here by foot?

August noticed my confusion and said, "This is our backyard. We like to raise and nurture trees as part of the local environmental program. They find and sometimes buy land. We help grow trees and donate our land for the cause. The house is up this way."

"But where is here?" I asked.

August giggles.

"I'll show you around tomorrow if you have the energy. Now you need to go see our father. Then you can rest," she said with a smile.

I decided not to argue. The word rest sounded too inviting. I don't even know what time it is, but I know I've been up for over fifteen hours. Likely more, depending on the walk. We came up to a well-kept Victorian-style house amongst the trees. Out of all the scary stories I have heard, I had a different picture of what a vampire's home would look like. Even though it is classy as I expected, it didn't look that old. I'll call out my bias on that one and color me surprised. It had a patio swing. I don't have many clear memories of my mother, but one that I do remember had a patio swing. It almost reminds me of the one my mother and I had. I remember it was a summer sunset with a warm wind blowing. I rested my head on my mother's lap as we swung, and she hummed a song. Hum...I think...no, it must be because of everything. I'm likely recreating memories that are not there, like a shadow moving in the tree that day.

3

The Familiar House

Again, August noticed my lack of presents and shook my shoulder to help me snap out of my thoughts. We were standing inside the Victorian house, and two new faces were looking at me. Both looked identical to August, with red hair, brown eyes, and relatively full-looking faces. The only exception was that these two had much longer hair than August's pixy haircut. One had her hair pulled back in a ponytail with a dark blue bow. She wore a simple white blouse and a long black skirt. She would look like a schoolteacher if she did not look so young. The other person's hair was loose and wild. She wore ripped blue jeans and a t-shirt with an angry rabbit.

"Roxanne, you're spacing out again," August said quietly.

"I'm sorry. I guess you were trying to introduce me to these two. Given their likeness with you, August, I'm also going to guess that these two are the sisters you mentioned earlier," I said with a tone of embarrassment.

"O', August told you about us?" the sister with the ponytail asked with a smile.

"Hard to believe that you would actually remember a conversation since you can't seem to stay focused for a simple greeting," the wild-looking sister retorted.

"I didn't say much about either of you. Only that we have sisters. Mostly we talked about her blood waking and some basic knowledge about vampires that she likely doesn't know being raised with a human's perception," August explained.

I take it gossiping about siblings isn't normal for them.

"We'll let me re-introduce myself," the person with the ponytail said, "My name is Julia. I am so happy we finally get to spend some time together. I hoped your blood would have woken up sooner, but it doesn't matter. It's awake now, and we can finally have some fun."

"Pleasure to meet you," I said.

I felt unsure how to take what she said. With my fatigue, I felt like I may have misunderstood something.

"Julia is our oldest sister, Roxanne. She has been a bit of a mother figure in our family since our biological mother died. I think she would've liked an opportunity to raise you herself after we learned your mother passed away, too," August explained.

"Okay, I think I see what you're saying. I suppose an eighteen-year-old could still be considered a child compared to a vampire," I said.

"For a full-blooded vampire, yes," Julia said, "However you're a half-vampire, so you could still be considered more of a pre-youth."

"Why is that?" I asked.

"Well, an average half-blood has a shorter life span than a full-blooded vampire. Since your body was born 'living,' it would likely wore down quicker than ours. You can still live much longer than any human by many centuries," Julia said with care.

I can tell that she has had time to practice this conversation. She really does give a motherly vibe, but it is not overbearing.

"I think August mentioned a case of a half-blood waking up at seventy-nine years old. Do we know if the life span was shorter because their body lived nearly a fully human life?" I asked.

Julia's eyes light up.

"I should've guessed that you would have questions like that. Your Aunt Madeline and Uncle Ernest are both scientists. They raised you to understand the importance of searching for comprehensible truths," Julia said with delight.

Then Julia grimly said, "Unfortunately, we don't know how long the person in the case actually could have lived. It's safe to say it would've been an even shorter time based on other cases."

I could tell Julia didn't care to talk about or think about the subject. She was trying to be as honest as possible with me despite her discomfort. The way she phrased 'actually could have lived' makes it sound like the person didn't die due to what they would consider natural causes. Perhaps it was due to the shock and disbelief. They could've died due to behavior-related causes.

"Thank you for sharing what you know about the case with me, Julia. I'm sorry if it made you uncomfortable to talk about. But I think I can see why the case would be considered inconclusive," I said.

She seemed upset that I had read between the lines of what she said.

"You don't have to worry about me, though. I might not understand everything and may have times of disbelief. Still, I'll not be as reckless about this new reality. I'll take adjusting one day at a time," I continued saying to help lessen her fear.

Julia seemed to relax. I think she was afraid hearing about the case could put ideas in my head. She didn't want me to die after waiting eighteen years for my blood to wake.

"Alright, so Julia is the oldest, and you are?" I asked, pointing to the wild-looking one.

"Why are you more interested in things unrelated to you?" the wild-looking one retorted.

Fair observation but rude. I'm trying to engage with you now. Julia was the one now retorting the wild one.

"It's how she had been raised as a human. It's how she bonded with her aunt and uncle," Julia tried to explain to the wild one.

Again, a fair observation, but I don't like being seen as rigid and orderly like my aunt and uncle.

"How did she ever make friends with that way of thinking?" the wild one asked.

Okay, now I'm feeling attacked. Over the last fourteen years, my lifestyle has been tight, and my friends took the time to learn who I am and not judge me based on how I think.

"Amelia, that's enough. Your sister asked you a question," A male voice said coming from the room in front of us.

My instinct told me it was a living room. The layout of the house feels familiar to me somehow. I can't put my finger on it. The voice is likely our dad's voice. He must have been listening to our conversation. I'll assume he has heard everything since August and I entered the house. The wild Amelia huffed and rolled her eyes at our father's order.

"It's okay. I think I have the general picture of which sibling you are," I said.

Amelia scoffed and said, "O' really?"

"Yep, you act more immature than Julia and August. Most people would assume you're the youngest, but you're not. You're the second child. As such, your behavior isn't a matter of maturity but of roles and responsibilities. Because Julia is the oldest daughter, she took over a parent's responsibility by looking after you and August as children. August, being assigned male at birth, has community-assigned responsibilities that came with the role of being a future clan leader. The only position left that has no responsibility expected is yours. Since no other siblings act like a child, that's your role. Also, judging from the sound in our father's voice, this is normal behavior for you to seek attention," I said reflectively.

Amelia was quiet for a moment but looked pissed. I think she is trying to think of a clever comeback to put me in my place.

"I know I'm younger, but I have no interest in competing with you. Besides, you and Julia have both been right on some accounts. I tend to think and talk like my aunt and uncle, which is off-putting for some people. I'm lucky that my friends accept me for the socially awkward person I am. They were willing to get to know me," I said, trying to defend myself from the earlier attack.

Amelia rolled her eyes and left. I don't think it will be easy to get along with her. Since she didn't correct me, I think I nailed the role and tension with the family structure. That does open the door to more questions that need to be asked. I can hardly think about that now. My body is telling me I'm beyond exhausted. If I must talk to him before I can rest, I should try to keep the conversation with him short. August tells me that she needs to be on her way if she wants to manage a fair hunt. Julia offered to straighten out my hair before I met dad.

"I have a quick question to ask if you don't mind, Roxanne," she said.

"I don't mind. Go ahead," I replied.

"How did you know it was father telling Amelia to answer your question?" Julia asked almost in a hushed tone.

"It was more of an assumption of mine than fact. I doubt anyone would talk to you three that way unless it was our father," I answered.

Since dad is a clan leader, I think a lower rank clan member would be more mindful of giving orders to their leader's child. The only exception I can think of would be if our father happened to grant permission to another due to Amelia's childish nature.

"I suppose that makes sense. I think you have a solid intuition given your age. Scientific minds like your aunt and uncle helped your intuition. Science provides a language to help explain what's second nature to you," she said sweetly, patting my head.

"You're the second person who commented on my intuition tonight. I am sure I can be right about some things, but even my intuition has blind spots. So, if I'm ever wrong or missing anything important, please feel free to let me know. That way, I can learn from my mistakes," I replied.

I must have said something to worry her. I think she wants to know what happened to make me say what I did, but I don't have it in me to talk about it now. Thankfully I think she is willing to let it go. She assured me that she would help me if I missed anything. Although she doubts that the need would arise. I thanked her and when to the living room to meet my dad.

I can't say for sure that I was surprised or if the living room was what I expected. The room was covered with wood worked details carefully crafted. That is normal for a Victorian house. The furnisher looked like refurbished antiques. There were bookshelf built-ins filled with books I had not heard of.

Some had missing labels due to frequent use or appeared to be entirely written in a different language. Perhaps old languages? Then a male voice greeted me.

"I figured you'd be tired of books after living with them. How often have you tried to go to places you know they would disapprove of?" A man with shoulder-length red curly hair asked.

He looked like he would be in his early-40s. Unlike my sisters and me, he had a slightly longer and thinner face with a petite nose. It shouldn't be surprising that his daughters look like teenagers. I need to remember age is almost irrelevant to them.

"I had to stop counting. It has only been since this summer that they finally loosened up being helicopter parents. Did I cause problems for you without knowing I was?" I asked.

I can't imagine what these past years were like for them.

"Compared to the places you could've gone, my dear Roxanne, you never really gave us any problems," he said thoughtfully.

"With that being said, where were you tonight? August couldn't find you," he asked.

I felt confused, likely because I didn't know how they had kept track of me. I supposed I should have asked August before she left or while we were walking here.

"I honestly don't know why August couldn't find me. I told my Aunt Madeline and Uncle Ernest my schedule for tonight. My friends and I kept it, apart from arriving at the movie's theater fifteen minutes late," I said.

From the look on his face, he must have not been informed of my schedule this evening or perhaps misinformed. It also looks like he will not ask what the schedule was. He just wants my story.

"I think you might what to know all of it," I said, feeling frustrated.

So much has happened, and I'm tired. Why did some pain in the butt have to go and lie to him?

He nods. Wonderful.

"Alright, at five P.M., my friends Damien, Penny, and Sasha had picked me up from my aunt and uncle's house. We went to a casino called House of Luck, which Penny's mom knows," I started to explain.

I think he doesn't want to know his daughter was at a casino. Nevertheless, it was my birthday. In our human tradition, I would be considered an adult.

"Then we went to see a horror film at the Dynamic Cinema. Like I said, we were a few minutes late. Lastly, we went to a club Damien's cousin, Bruce, works at to finish the night. And my blood woke at the club," I said, wanting to get the conversation over with.

My father raised his hand but clearly not to ask a question. He was likely gesturing for me to stop so he could think about something he heard.

"You went to Night's Spring Club?" he said or asked.

I really couldn't tell if he wanted an answer or not. So, I nodded.

I would ask how he knew based on Damien's cousin's relationship, but he likely knows more things than I do. I can't really think that far about how this rabbit hole could lead.

"I see," he said, "Then you met your relatives?"

" I did meet Kalt, but I don't know any other relatives. He only briefly mentioned his mother. I haven't met her," I said.

He was still silent at this.

I can't guess what he is thinking. I know Kalt had been a jerk to his child. Still, is there something he is not telling me that I should be worried about? I feel like there is something, but I don't know if it's bad or natural from his expression. It's clearly not good. It would be nice to know if I was in danger while being there.

"Alright, I think I understand what happened this evening. I know you have been through a lot and are tired. Your room is upstairs, second door to your right," he said.

A pause, and he sighs.

"I see you are not content. It seems Julia and Kalt are right about your intuition. It's normal for vampires to be keenly aware of potential threats. Nevertheless, it is impressive that you've had this keen ability for a few years while being human. Like your mother, you can get into trouble someday if you can't keep your wits in check with those you deal with. Playing your trump card early can lead to future problems. I have nothing concrete to share. Your intuition is picking up on a few theories I have. I would rather not say anything till I know for sure," he said.

I guess I'm easy to read for him. That sucks.

"I do have one more question for you before I go. This house's layout feels...." I started to say.

He smiled.

"I hoped you would remember it. I thought moving our family into your mother's house would be helpful for you when you woke. Your sisters don't seem to mind the change. They even helped prepare your room," he explained with more joy in his voice than earlier.

"Bet two out of three were content with that," I said sarcastically.

"Give Amelia time to warm up to you," he said, "Now, to bed. It will be a challenging few days as you get used to being a vampire, my Roxanne. I know it will take time, but I need you to be on our schedule before being presented to the council in eight days."

"Why do I need to be presented to the council?" I asked.

"The population of our types is off since you woke this year. The other two types need to be made aware and decide how and whom will have the opportunity to increase their population. It can be considered an exciting time yet very political. It can bring some tensions to the surface. I am legally required to provide proof. My proof that your blood woke is to bring you," he explained, "I'm sure you heard plenty about the council and our type for one day. Get some rest, my child."

With that, Julia came into the space and helped escort me to my room. I didn't know how tired I was. Julia offered to share her amulet's energy with me since I didn't, in their perspective, consume as much as I should have. Her amulet almost resembled a flower with petals etched into the stone. I tried to let her keep it, but she was surprisingly persistent and assured me that she could always get more energy later. She also argued that I would feel miserable and sickly even after resting if I didn't eat properly. I ate, and it was still an uncomfortable feeling of being shocked. Julia helped explain more about feeding and a few tricks that help infants eat. Even for full-blood vampires, the experience is not pleasant. It can be hard to encourage newborns to eat. She told me to try those suggestions to help make eating more tolerable for me. Then I quickly fell asleep. That ends my 18th birthday and possibly my first re-birthday.

4

For Science and Restless Sleep

Even with four months, where I could sleep in and stay up as late as I wanted, I never did. I was more comfortable going about my days as if life hadn't changed after graduating high school and living with my aunt and uncle. I'm starting to wonder whether it would've been easier for me if I should have tested those waters more. I found it a shock to my senses to be in an unfamiliar room when I woke. Despite being up past midnight, I can see the light around the edges of my curtains. That would mean that the sun is up in the sky. I know I didn't check to see what time I went to bed. I don't see a clock in my room to tell me what time it is now.

I felt hazy as I tried to search the room. It could be that I am tired still, but it could be again due to not being able to eat my new food well. I think Julia called it that I would. It would help to know what time it was. I could've woken up at nine. If it's later, that would probably be better since I will need to learn to stay awake at night. But such is my habit. I'm used to other morning routines that would likely kill me now.

The first thing I almost tried to do to find out the time was to open the curtains. Thankfully, my body seemed to have a mind of its own and froze up as my hand neared the rope that drew back the curtains. I found it odd that my body should simply stop on its own. I became thankful when I realized how fatal that decision would have been. I then went to turn on a light switch, and the same sudden body freeze happened again. I had to stop and think for a moment. I plopped down on my bed to think, which did not feel pleasant. It felt like getting a car tire to move while stuck in a ditch. Okay, last night, the lights were on in the hallway, and a fire in the fireplace. It could be uncomfortable to be around certain lights, but I don't think they would use any in this house. I should be able to turn the light switch on.

I then tried again and found myself able to flip the switch. So, my instinct of self-preservation will kick in when I am about to do something I have not thought through fully that could be fatal to me. That's good but a pain in a pinch. Not seeing a clock, I decided to turn off the lights. It might be good for me to get used to dark places and be able to see in the dark. I also would want to try one more test. The problem is I don't want to hurt myself if I am right.

How do I test the working theory that my body only freezes when I have not thought through a potentially dangerous action? I could tell myself that sunlight from the window would not kill me, but I know that is likely not the case. Could I say that it is unlikely that the curtains will not hurt me if I touch them? The layer facing the room should have less contact with sunlight than the other layers. It should be alright for me to touch that part of the curtain. I reach my hand out, and I feel my body tensing up and trying to freeze on me. Still, I could touch the curtain, and it felt like what I would imagine touching a hot stovetop would feel like. I checked my hand, and I did not see any sign of burns or other damage done to my skin. I checked to see if my hand felt sensitive, and it did not seem so. Okay, it will not hurt me, but it is something I should try to avoid doing unless of an emergency. The fact that I am half-blood could help explain why it may not hurt as much. Could it be that it could take time for sunlight to affect me more than others? I wonder.

How to test that without harm? I began to play with my hair as I pondered this question. After a few moments of playing, I noticed a strand of hair loosened. Hmm. That could work. If I could break the hair, I could try leaving it in sunlight to see what happens and how fast if anything happens to it. I could also look for strands of loose hair to test from the others. I will also want to find a way to move the hair to the sunlight without getting close myself. And perhaps something that would not take in the heat from the sunlight easily.

I started looking around my room for loose hair or anything that could help me place the hair in the sunlight. Again, it was no simple task since my mind was still in a bog. Hmm.

No hairs, at least that I can see in the dark. I may have found a few things that could help move the hair in place for the test from the vanity. However, I don't know how much sunlight the objects will take in. I sigh. I took a moment to think things over. Is it possible to move the strand of hair into the sunlight while still being close to the shadows? If I do that, I will not be able to break the hair for more experiments; I will have to wait for another strand to fall out. Okay, I will use this strand of hair to see what happens. I will keep my hand as far away from the window's ledge. I thread the hair towards the sunlight. If it doesn't work, I'll think of a plan B.

With that, my sunlight experiment took place. I ran my strand of hair along the wall till it was on the sunny side of the curtains. Because I couldn't move the curtains to see what was happening to the hair on the other side, I counted to five seconds when I felt half of the strand of hair should be exposed to the sunlight. I would then pull out the strand and observe any changes compared to my healthy hair in the vanity mirror. After I counted five seconds, I pulled the hair out from the other side of the curtains. It didn't look like a noticeable change had occurred. I then went to the mirror to compare; it looked fine with no noticeable changes. I then tried the same experiment with the same hair three more times, and nothing changed. I then change the amount of time to ten seconds.

When nothing seemed to change again, I knew I needed a better method of keeping time. At least a split second of sunlight will not kill me if this attempted test is correct. I now know that sunlight can be at the very least painful, even when not exposed. It would be better to have different strands, though, to compare. It would also be nice to know what time of day it is. That way, I can determine if this window was getting full or partial sunlight. I think everyone's still asleep, though.

I was physically starting to feel tired, but I knew I wouldn't rest easy without a clear answer to this question, even with my muddled mind. O' well. I need to rest while it is daytime. I think my family gave me the grace to sleep last night since I was up all day. They will likely want me to be up all night tonight because I have had an opportunity to sleep all day today. It will likely take a few days for me to adjust. I think it's safe to say I will have a few more mornings to try my experiments. If anything, hopefully, there will be a time when I'll not have to worry about my father's rules and expectations. Even vampires would want their children to leave home sometime. Hmm... I forgot to ask how old the other three are and what age is considered an adult. Since I am still considered a pre-youth. With a head full of wonder, I fell back to sleep. Before my mind drifted away, I thought to myself, 'I should've read to pass the time.'

Again, I woke up sometime later. This time because nature called. Interesting, I thought that function wouldn't be necessary as a sound vampire. It's only been a few hours since my blood woke. I went almost intuitively to where the bathroom would likely be in the house. For not living here in the last fourteen years, it's amazing that I still can safely guess where everything would be. I never thought I was that observant as a child.

After tending to my personal business, I thought of the bookshelves in the living room. I don't recall dad saying that I couldn't read a book from there. I went to my room and grabbed a pillow and blanket to take with me. I used to do the same thing in my uncle's study. Uncle Ernest never minded me reading his books but was constantly upset with me for taking them out of his workspace. Often the book I would be reading was one he needed for work, and he felt it a hassle to constantly go into my room to retrieve it. He told me to camp out in his office when I wanted to read one of his books. Since I don't know if dad would be upset with me taking a book from a shelf to read, it seems safe to continue the camp method. When I went to the living room, I set up a corner next to the bookshelves and picked out a faded purple cover book. The writing on the cover was worn, but the letters were in good condition despite the age. I started reading the book.

After a few lines, I learned that it is a book about past wars, genocides, and the creation of the known social taboos in vampire culture laced with many politics. I have never been a history buff, but I am curious about my new reality. Especially if I want to be able to become independent again. Knowing nothing about them and wanting to be independent could likely lead to harm. I don't blame them for wanting to keep an eye on me and educate me. Guiding me and all of this. It is such a setback for me to think about, though. I was so close to being independent and having a life of my own now that I find myself no better than a child again. I put those thoughts aside and focused my attention on the book. From time to time, I would take a break to stretch. The wood floor, after a while, can be uncomfortable. I did find a clock hanging over the door frame to the hallway. I did not notice it last night. Likely because I had plenty on my mind. It reads 3:46 P.M. I should probably try sleeping again as I looked back to the book. I have already finished reading half of it.

I have never heard of the wars mentioned in the book since most are between the three types. Some of the fights also involved humans: vampire hunters. The genocides are just as bad as the Globle Wars, I studied in high-school. However in this book, both people and vampires were test subjects. As a result, social taboos were created to maintain harmony and equality. It'd help prevent further harm and create new breeds of vampires learned from past experiments. According to the book, those who became new breeds had power, which was something to be feared. Hence, their existence had to be erased to maintain safety for the dominant race of vampires and the rest of human and animal populations alike.

The taboo most mentioned in the book was consuming the life energy of another vampire. Honestly, I never thought that a vampire would feed on another. I thought I was safe. To be fair, I didn't know vampires existed outside of scary stories. I thought I was safe as a human too. Unaware that I could've been some vampires' meal. Before I could dwell more on the subject, I went asleep again, this time in my little camp corner.

My dreams are odd. Where most people dream of flying or teeth falling out, my dreams tend to be forgettable or memories of past events. I was awakened again by a memory from talking with Kalt about his family. The pause I thought was anxiety, only later to learn that he was eating in front of me. I thought it was his way of helping, but a chill ran up my back and caused me to wake up. Could Kalt be redirecting an urge to feed on me before my blood woke? I didn't feel like I was in danger then, but my body is now curling up in a ball at the thought.

I felt a hand on my back. I jumped due to fear. I looked around to find that dad was trying to comfort me. I did not know anyone was awake, but I suppose since it was close to evening. I apologized for the jump, and he assured me it was fine.

"I can imagine, after everything, it would be normal to have nightmares," he said warmly.

I felt he should know that my mind's way of dreaming was odd. It wasn't a nightmare as much as a reinterpretation of memory due to what I had been reading. He asked about the memory and the book I was reading. I handed over the book and explained my memory of talking to Kalt about his family. That Kalt seemed uncomfortable and bit his bloodstone.

"This book would give any person nightmares," my father reassured me.

Yet he did not seem convinced. Dad can be a hard person to read, but it will not surprise me if he knows more about the type of person Kalt really was. Dad promises me that I am safe and that the family will not let anything bad happen to me. Yet, despite this assurance, I can't help but wonder. Is Kalt that type of person who would be tempted to try a taboo?

Seeing me still unconvinced and questioning the dream, my dad started a conversation.

"Kalt, August, and I are all entrusted into a privileged and frightening role. We create and enforce the governing laws of all vampires in our region. We help keep our world in balance and uphold the dignity and rights of all. We ensure that the evolution and the creation of even stronger nightmares don't occur in our world," he started to say.

Dad paused and walked over to the chair he sat in last night with the book I was reading.

"Come sit next to me, my Roxanne," father said.

He gestured to a chair. I went over and took a seat beside him.

"You have heard a lot about human wars while in school. I know that you had a rather prickly political history teacher in the eleventh grade who had mentioned the economic benefits of war to you and your peers. Let me impart my words of wisdom on the subject from experiences and help explain to you that everything has a cost. Even when the benefits are desirable. The larger question should always be asked is whether it is ever worth the cost? The book you read is one that every council member and future council member must read and know by heart," he said.

I felt fear and shame.

"Am I in trouble for reading that book then?" I asked with concern.

He chuckled.

"No, anyone can read it. Most people wouldn't want to if they could avoid it. As you can tell, it's not a pleasant read and shows a lot of our dark history. Inhumanity is in its very nature. After all, whether we want to accept it, vampires are nightmares to humankind and ourselves if left unchecked and without humility. Vampires, from our understanding, are a byproduct of inhumane behaviors at the expense of other people's lives and dignity. Unlike the minor evolutions over time in life, what created us wasn't a favorable evolution. It's out of greed, pride, or selfish desires at great cost and unredeemable losses. With all due respect, your teacher will never know the true value of human life that only one chance to live. A life that could've changed our world for the better. At the expense of hate and greed that only war has to offer. The money they'll always have with them could be earned in many ways far fairer than war," he said with a mix of frustration and disappointment.

He paused, needing another moment of silence.

"I am thankful that you're curious about our world. I want you to have the freedom to explore it to your heart's content. I want the same for your sisters. Kalt isn't our favorite person nor his mother. They both have not shown respect to our family in ways we prefer. However, they should have sense enough as extended family to you not to harm you. And as council members, not to act on our legal taboos," he said.

"I see," I said, reflecting on how foolish my nightmare was.

"You haven't been a vampire for more than a day, my dear Roxanne. You only met your cousin briefly. I can only imagine how fearful our world would seem at first. Your fear isn't misplaced. It's only doing its best to keep you safe and alive," he said in a caring tone.

It seemed that he wanted to say more but stopped. I don't think he wants me to worry about things I haven't learned yet.

"With all this being said, don't feel ashamed telling me about the things you learn. Please don't feel like you have to hide anything from me. I may disapprove of some of your choices, like this book. However, I want to help you understand that our world might not seem so sunny and safe. Yet it should be a world where you feel like you can be yourself and thrive," dad said.

August walked into the living room as I thanked dad.

"Morning, father. Roxanne, how did you sleep? Are you hungry?" August asked.

"I can't say I slept great, but I got some sleep. As for hungry, I don't know. I know it's been several hours since I last ate, but I don't feel hungry. I also feel like most of our conversation starts with food," I said, trying to lighten the mood.

August replied, "We have to ask if you're hungry a lot because of your past association of feeling hungry compared to your new experience with hunger. When you were alive, your body would let you know with growing sounds and cravings, among other ways, I'm sure. Now your body will not tell you that you're hungry the same way. You don't eat because you feel like it. You eat to prevent feeling weak, tired, or sick. You eat pure energy, and you use that energy. You need to eat or sleep when your energy starts to feel drained. Although sleep can also do little to restore your energy since your body still uses energy while you sleep. That is why we try to eat well to afford to sleep well. Also, eating isn't a pleasant experience. I know it is something you may be tempted to write off. That is why Julia and I will insist that you eat regularly. To us, you're like a newborn who needs a regular feeding schedule whether you like it or not."

I understand where she is coming from, but it sounds like a pain. I haven't felt well since I woke up the first time. I suppose I didn't eat well before bed if what August said is true.

"I understand, and I think I am hungry," I said reluctantly.

"Good. I have plenty of food for us this morning. You'll need plenty of energy to learn how to hunt today," August says with a grin.

"I'm confused. Do we need to hunt daily? If you collected enough, why would we need more?" I asked.

"A sound stone can hold a day's worth of food for one person. A vampire who can eat without their stone through passive hunting can manage to make the daily amount in their stone last longer. Since we need to shear our stone's food with you, we will need to hunt with more intention and frequently to help keep everyone well fed," August explained.

"You mentioned passive hunting. What is the difference between hunting and passive hunting?" I asked.

"The only difference between the two is need," father said.

He seemed happy to be a part of a conversation about how our family does things. I can imagine our earlier conversation would have felt more work-related tensions. I get the feeling being a parent brings him joy. Being able to raise his children means more than his position as a member of the council.

"When we talk about hunting, we often refer to the need for energy and intentionally seek our meal out. When we passively hunt, we are around and have easy access to energy but may not have an immediate need to consume it. Yet we gather or eat it since it is available," father continued.

"I think I understand," I said, "It still seems to me that passive hunting is more pleasant the having to be actively hunting. I do feel bad putting you all through this."

August takes her shark tooth-looking amulet out and puts it in my hand.

"You're not putting us through anything we didn't expect. We want to help you adjust and thrive. So, stop procrastinating and eat your fill this morning. Julia had told you a few tricks to help. We will have plenty of time to practice passive eating and hunting today," August said, trying to act like a parent.

The word hunting bothers me, and I feel I would look like a fool trying. For that reason, I tried to use one of Julia's suggestions for eating. I need to make sure I eat well, so I don't make a fool of myself later. I could end up sick if tonight doesn't go well. I take a bite. I recalled what Julia suggested. I try not to focus on the energy while eating but on my body. To think of my body as a bag of water and the energy like waves moving the water. It doesn't feel like electricity but like waves in still water. The waves don't hurt; water only moves in motion. I need to be willing to invite with my sense of self and let the waves fill me. I did feel relief from my bog. I am still unsure whether I am eating well enough to get through this night. I give the amulet back to August.

"It's still early for my liking. We will hang out here until ten-thirty," August said.

Then she bit her amulet and pulled up a chair on my other side. Dad pats my head and thanks me for eating well. He put up the book I was reading and grabbed the one he was working on last night. I wonder what their normal routine is like.

Before I could ask what a typical day for them is, August asked me, "Are you really going to wear that same outfit for another day? You do have clean clothes in your room. We bought them for you in advance if you woke up this year. They should fit."

I looked down. I have been wearing the same outfit for hours and didn't even think about changing. Both August and dad were already dressed for the day. August was wearing simple sleaves top blue and white striped top with a deep dark blue frilly skirt at knee length and black boots that covered any socks she wore. Dad wore a black dress shirt, blue dress pants, and brown leather shoes.

"I didn't know. I looked around my room earlier when I woke up. But I still have not looked through my dresser or closet," I said thoughtfully.

"Then how about finding a cute outfit for you to go on your first hunt in," August said with joy.

5

Hair

We headed for my room. August couldn't wait to show me the clothes the family had bought for me in anticipation of my blood waking this year. I do feel a bit awkward. I never really paid attention to the details of the space. I only noticed a few things in the room between my arrival and searching for some tools in the dark. I knew there was a full bed, a vanity, a closet, a wardrobe, and a chest full of stuffed animals. Or at least some soft fabrics which could have been pillows. There were boxes under the bed with papers and books. I couldn't say what types of books were in the boxes or what was soft in the chess. The vanity had tweezers, a hairbrush, jars, and nail trimers set out to find with ease. Inside the vanity's drawer were lots of small boxes. August turned on the lights in my room. I can now see what I had missed while searching in the dark.

The bed was a full-sized bed. I was used to sleeping on a twin-sized bed while living with my aunt and uncle. When I arrived last night, I didn't notice that this bed was old and made of wood. Its headboard had a simple floral design etched in with care. It had a netted curtain to make it look more privet than the intended design. It could've been added to keep bugs away as I slept. But I doubt that's the case with how well kept the house is. The blanket and sheets were different shades of purple. The bed skirt was dusk pale pink. The vanity and the vanity's chair were the only pieces of furniture in the room made of metal. Some of the detailed floral work on the vanity and its chair are painted black and white. It could be a design choice to help lessen the amount of reflected light in the room. The carpet was deep dark gray. The walls were painted a deep rich red. I could not tell if it was to represent theater curtains or blood. The rest of the dark-stained wood furniture was antique woodwork pieces that were well cared for.

August went straight for the closet and opened the doors. Inside it was full of clothes I would consider formal attire. There were black velvet skirts like what Julia had worn the night before. Some white blouses with little lacework. The rest of the blouses, pants, skirts, jackets and business coats were plain, dark, and rich in color. Nothing in this closet said gothic or playful person. The dresses are the most interesting pieces in the closet. Despite not being my style, I will say that it is still better than looking like a fast-food employee. Before I knew it, August pulled out an outfit she wanted me to wear today.

"Here, this will be absolutely perfect for your first hunt!" August beamed with delight. She had in her hands a dark green sleeveless dress with a black ribbon belt tied into a bow on the right side. August put the dress in my hand and immediately went back into the closet.

"What else are you looking for?" I asked, "And can I really hunt in a dress like this?"

August seemed to be looking at a small collection of boots and pulled out a pair of black strap-woven sandals.

She handed them to me and replied to my questions with, "I was looking for these cute shoes. Best to enjoy them while the weather isn't quite cold. A dress like this is a treat for the eyes."

August managed to drag me into the bathroom to get dressed while explaining, "That dress will also encourage social activity around us by attracting some types of extroverted people. Suppose we attract humans who're willing to be social around us. In that case, it creates less work on our part to be socially engaged in conversation to collect food. The last thing I want to do is talk to people when my energy is low, and I haven't eaten. Naturally, different clothes attract different levels of social groups. Looking like you have been out to a club or bar can attract more extroverted people or social drunks. Let them do the talking to impress. You are free to listen or leave if you don't want to engage in conversation. It doesn't have to cost you a lost meal."

I finished getting changed by the end of her explanation. I opened the bathroom door to see a smile on her face.

"Are we going to a club to hunt then?" I said unenthusiastically.

August smiled.

"No, but people will think we are with the right look. All we have to do is walk around town and collect the living energy of the nightlife," she said.

She seemed to be looking for something else now.

Then she continued, "I think we can be good for a lap around Riggy Park and back. You can focus on what you're able to do tonight. Practicing your feeding technique of taking in energy around you is a good goal for today. Then I want to teach you how we can use living energy to do some fun things before we get home."

It felt like August wanted to surprise me by not saying anything more on the subject.

"What are you looking for?" I finally asked.

"I'm looking for Julia," August said.

"Why?" I asked, feeling confused.

"Julia has a talent for cutting hair," August said, "I checked her room this morning, but she was not there. I didn't see her downstairs while you were talking to our father. Seriously, where could she be?"

I still felt confused about why I needed my hair cut. I had my last haircut a month ago. I don't think it has gotten that long. It's still on the short side. I hate feeling so confused about what is going on around me. Lately, I feel like I am asking more questions than having actual conversations. I know it's a new world for me. Should I just take some time to watch and observe? Perhaps if I wait a while and watch, things will make more sense.

When we did find Julia, she was outside checking the mailbox.

"Where were you?!" August snapped. "I've been looking for you all morning."

"I'm sorry if I worried you both," Julia said sweetly and patted my head like a child.

"You look very nice today, Roxanne. August has planned to show you how to hunt for energy in easy social pools. It might seem intimidating to feed around a large crowd. Still, you'd be surprised how many humans overlook our presents in them. We just need to be around them and use our feeding techniques. Like the one I told you about last night," she shared in her usual motherly manner.

Julia looked over to August.

"I know you'll have her back if she has a hard time with any social anxieties," Julia said.

August looked upset at Julia and said, "Of course, I'll look after Roxanne. But you didn't answer my question; where were you this morning?"

Julia avoided the question and looked back at me.

"I should help get your hair done, Roxanne. Not that it's bad. Nevertheless, people might ask you many unwanted questions since your blood woke up. Like, where you went off to?" Julia said sweetly.

August seemed to notice the slight hint in Julia's remark and scowled.

Julia said, "It's best if you don't look too much like yourself. It'd be hard to explain the truth. With that said, what type of hairstyle do you like best? A pixie cut like August's hair. I can make a messy bob with curls. However, it'd mean that you'll have to take time to curl your hair during the mornings. What do you think you would like?"

"If you really want to go the extra mile, you can ask Julia for a buzz cut," August retorted, clearly upset with Julia.

"Julia has had to cut my hair many times and has mastered the request for a buzz cut," August continued hotly.

"I'm glad you enjoyed them. All I can say is that I try to do my best," Julia replied in her usual sweet tone.

I think she knew why August was upset. Yet she still had no interest in sharing.

"Since Roxanne has an important choice to make, how about you be so kind as to share the story of where you've been this morning, Julia. While she decides?" August asked.

"How about nobody cares where Julia's been this morning, August," Amelia yelled from the front door frame.

She looked like she had only recently gotten out of bed. She was still in what looked like a nightgown. It's hard to tell if she had a bedhead considering her hair was just as messy the night before. I started wondering if the nightgown was a hammy down. It seemed different than the style I would safely assume she would prefer to wear. It seemed more of what I would expect Julia would ware. It also seemed odd that Amelia would butt her head into her sisters' dispute. It could come from her playing the role of the youngest sibling. Either she dislikes it when their positions of responsibility clash, or she just wants to add her frustration to theirs.

"Amelia!" Julia exclaimed, "Your hair is a mess. How about we get your hair combed? You can share with us what your plans are for today. Since we already can tell what these two are going to do. And Roxanne will have time to think about what she wants."

Amelia made a face.

"Don't you dare come near me with a comb! You will not touch my hair! It always hurts when you comb my hair. I am not your scapegoat!" Amelia said, heading back inside the house.

"Come on! It will just take a moment! Your hair will feel lighter after it gets untangled," Julia said with a voice of delight, chasing Amelia into the house.

Julia really does not want to answer August's question.

I wonder if she uses her parental duties to deflect personal questions often. I'd feel bad for Amelia. Yet she chose to be a part of the conflict by defending Julia's privacy. I wonder how long it will take for Julia to comb Amelia's hair.

I also wonder what kind of hairstyle I'd want. I have never had much choice. It was either long hair or bowl cut. In fifth grade and beyond, I got stuck with bowl cuts. Probably because I picked that style too often. Before that, my aunt would've kept my hair long, and I only had it trimmed. A bowl cut back then felt so much lighter and different. I felt more inclined to pick it. August's pixie haircut isn't bad, but I don't want people to get confused about who is who. All four of us can look the same. I can only tell Julia and Amelia apart because Amelia's hair is a mess, and Julia keeps her hair up. If they did nothing but comb their hair, I would not be able to tell them apart based on appearance.

I think I still want to do something different. A hard no on the buzz cut. I might have an edgy side, but ...wait a moment. I think a mohawk, but the hair in the center is not standing up. It can fall on one side or another with a shorter possible buzzed cut on either side without being too short. It can be reversible if I want the long hair to fall all on the left or right side. That could be fun. I'll run this by Julia.

"Earth to Roxanne. Are you in there, Roxanne?" August said.

I must have seemed like I was spacing out again.

"O' sorry, August. I did not mean to get lost in my thoughts again. I was just thinking about what I wanted to do with my hair. Was there something you wanted to talk about?" I asked, feeling embraced.

August sighed and said, "That was what I was trying to ask you about. If you had any ideas about what you want to do with your hair."

"I think I do. I'd like to know how short Julia's buzz cuts are first. I don't want it to be super short. It would be nice to have some length," I replied.

August's eyes grew. Her mouth gaped open.

"You knew I was giving Julia a hard time talking about the buzz cuts earlier. Right?" August asked.

"Yes. But if Julia can, I'd like to see if she can make a very flattering and fun style with some buzz cut help," I said with a tone of delight at the thought.

August looked at me, horrified. I didn't know how to explain it. If I try to explain it to Julia, she might know what the style is that I'm thinking about. I went inside the house to look for Julia. It didn't take me long to find her. I found her in the kitchen brushing the hair of a very reluctant Amelia.

"Hey Julia, how many types of hairstyles do you know? I've got an idea of what I would like, but I don't know the style," I said when I saw her.

It seemed I had interrupted a conversation the two were having without noticing. Amelia looked pissed. Julia stopped combing Amelia's hair. Her hair looked longer being straightened out than when it's a mess.

"Good timing. I've just finished combing Amelia's hair. Our Amelia will be helping the young men at Port 74 with checking our clan's imports today," Julia said in her usual sweet tone.

Amelia just realized that Julia had stopped combing her hair. She got up from her stole and bolted out of the kitchen with a huff.

"Okay, that leaves me with questions," I said.

Julia smiled and replied, "Well, we'll have time before your first hunt. Now, what were you thinking about doing with your hair?"

I told her what I was thinking. While explaining the style, August showed up with our dad beside her. Julia reflected for a moment. Then she pulled out her smartphone to do a quick search.

"Is this what you were thinking about? I think it's similar and complements your dress. It's called a pixie mohawk," Julia asked.

I looked at the pictures.

"It doesn't look exactly like what I had in mind. But I think this looks much nicer than what I was thinking about. I like this style. Do you think that you can do something like this?" I asked.

"I will do my best. I don't think it will take too long," Julia said.

Julia handed her phone over to our father. That way, he might see the hairstyle we are talking about. August looked over his shoulder to see the pictures. I think August told dad I was planning to ruin my hair with a crazy hairstyle. They seemed relieved after seeing the pictures. Without waiting for their approval, Julia started working on my hair. She began to explain what Port 74 is and what types of imports arrived there. She also explained why Amelia would be going there today.

"Let me see if I got this right. Sound stones are manufactured. I thought it's a rare natural stone," I said with surprise.

"I know Madeline and Ernest don't work in earth sciences. However, I figured you would know more about artificially made stones, Roxanne," Julia said.

She sounded surprised that there were things that I didn't know about.

"I have heard of artificially made diamonds, but that's it," I said.

"Still, the imported materials needed to craft sound stones go to Port 74," I continued reflecting aloud. I was trying to wrap my mind around this discovery.

Then I said, "I suppose it'd make sense that the stones would need to be replaced if they're used regularly. It's just that they look solid to me."

" There's also a demand for more stones when new sound vampires are born," Julia said.

She takes a moment from working on my hair to adjust herself in her seat to get a better angle.

"We expect your sound stone to be crafted during this latest batch. That way, you can have some more room to be independent. I can imagine it can be frustrating to rely on others. You've had to adjust to our schedules and plans," Julia continued to say.

I still can't imagine what a typical day looks like for them after everything. Everything they do seems to be focused on helping me, directly or indirectly. I'm sure that they have more responsibilities than caring for me. Maybe that is why Julia doesn't want to share what she was doing this morning. She deserves to have some time just for herself. Not always being at the family's beck and call to take care of me.

"I'm curious. Since August and I will be going hunting. Amelia will check on the supplies needed to make sound stones. What are you going to be doing today? If you don't mind me asking," I ask, feeling awful.

Except I wanted to know if she could have a typical day.

"I don't mind telling you, Roxanne. After all, it will be something you'll likely have an opportunity to do someday, too," Julia said genitally with a hint of sadness in her voice.

She switched from scissors to a fine-tooth comb.

"Where to start?" she said, "I'm at an age now where I would be considered an adult. I turned 2000 years old this late summer. I'm also old enough to consider marriage proposals. I could also propose an offer to a person who is also old enough to be married. I can reject marriage offers until I feel ready. During this council meeting where you'll be presented, I will be expected to present my marriage proposal. During that time, I can be offered proposals of marriage by others. It's all done during the council for population control. It's to help them know who is married and who will likely be asking for an opportunity to have a child in the future."

She seems unsettled talking about it. After August coming out to the council, I imagine it's not a pleasant experience. To discuss personal matters in front of people who could choose to reject your desires and hopes for the future. I wonder if I should be concerned with being presented to them. Julia continues talking after she hands me a mirror.

"I'll be talking with father about it and ask for his guidance. He is a good person to talk to on the matter. He is the only member who has the longest history of remaining single. I can't help but think about what my mother told me. Apparently, when he presented his marriage offer before the councils, they never could find a reason to deny his request," Julia said with a sound of joy.

Hearing Julia talk about her mother raised some questions in my mind. I can't help but wonder what it must have been like for our dad to request to the council the right to marry my mother. I can't help but feel that there would be a lot of push-back. For him to marry a person who would be considered a meal. I looked in the mirror. First, I noticed my hair which looked fantastic. Then I moved the mirror to see Julia's face. She looked troubled. Her eyes were glassy. I felt worried for her. I want Julia to be happy and for things to go well. Looking back at myself in the mirror, I noticed something I should have noticed sooner.

"Hey, Julia? Why do we have reflections?" I asked with concern.

My question seemed to surprise Julia. Then she started to have a laughing fit.

It took her a few moments to collect herself before getting out, "Th...That's... a miss conception...humans have...about us."

After her fit of laughter, she continued to explain.

"I'm truly sorry for laughing. I've always wondered why no humans have ever questioned the logic of that myth themselves. They know a skeleton has a reflection, and zombies have also been thought to have reflections. Even though our bodies aren't living in a traditional sense, we are still considered under the same classification as the living dead. I should explain the logic behind the myth to you. Nowadays, it's a pointless method of hunting. The missing image in the mirror illusion depends on who we hunt and how we hunt in specific situations. When the illusion was invented, it was due to humans' religious debate on images. I think the time frame was called the Reformation period. If not a few years before the reformation. A particular infected vampire who had turned invented this branch of vanishing illusion. It was out of mockery of their opposing faith tradition. The illusion created fear in humans during that time. That fear enriched the adrenaline in the blood and the energy behind a human scream. It became a common practice that only lasted one hundred years. The fad, one could say, ended with the creator if they managed to live the full life of an infected vampire. Although given the time frame, that was not likely the case. It's been over four centuries since anyone needed to use that illusion. If it is used, it's only to create fear. I doubt many humans today would fall to the fear behind the illusion," Julia said in a brighter tone.

I was not expecting to see Julia's mood change so quickly.

"Okay, there is a trick to not having a reflection. It had to do with creating fear during the hunt," I said to reflect with Julia.

"Yep, we can use the living energy we gather to do many interesting things. It can vary from a simple illusion trick to a transformation. It's rare for some vampires to do something beyond those two. We don't need parlor tricks to hunt. We do transformations in a pinch. That's what August will begin teaching you tonight after your hunt. Now, what do you think about your hair, Roxanne?" Julia asked.

I had to look in the mirror again.

"I couldn't have imagined anything better. Thank you for the new look, Julia!" I said with a smile.

I couldn't believe that I was looking at myself in the mirror. Not once could I have imagined looking so different from the person I was a day ago? Sure, I tried to rebel. Except I would've always been too scared to desire to look this way living with my aunt and uncle. After all, they chose to take me in when I had no one. I probably could have ended up with that nightmare of a foster for much longer or worse. I still wonder and worry if my new family might abandon me. I just got here, but it sounds like a lot of change will come our way. Julia might be married. August is a council member in training. She is also a teacher and caretaker for me. Amelia wants nothing to do with me. Dad, it feels like my relationship with him is alright but complicated. It could be even more complex depending on how the council responds to our personal changes as a family. Could the council decide that I can't live with my family? Would I be expected to fend for myself in a world I thought I knew, but I don't know anything anymore?

Before my mind could wander down that dark road any further, I hear August yell, "Holy song! You look amazing, Roxanne! Julia's skills never cease to amaze."

Did she really say holy song? This is one time I feel I'd learn more from observing than asking. Julia thanked August for the over-exaggerated compliment while heading to a trashcan. She throughout the hair collection on the comb and hair trimmings. I think Amelia's strands of hair are in that mess, too.

I'll make a mental note for tomorrow's science experiment. For now, I need to learn everything I can about my new reality.

"August, I have to ask, is it time to go hunting yet?" I asked, feeling a need to learn.

6

The Hunt Begins

August was surprised but smiled.

"I think it's time to get going. But I'm curious why you're raring to go hunting. Are you starting to feel hungry already?" August said, placing a hand on my head.

"Remember the tricks I told you about yesterday, and you'd be able to eat well," Julia said, chiming in before heading out of the kitchen with her belongings in hand.

She now sounded more like herself than she had a moment ago.

"Well, Roxanne. Shall we head out?" August asked, sounding like I was the one slowing her down.

"Just one more look in the mirror, then we can go on our way," I teased back.

August smiled and seemed glad I was willing to play with her remark.

"Well, stop the presses. I think this sister of mine is vane. Can't blame you, though. Julia is the best when it comes to making the family look good," August playfully said.

"Why not ask for a touch of her magic for yourself before going," I responded to her play.

"I love Julia's magic, but it's best for special occasions. As for my everyday magic, I'm still fine-looking." August said, practically waltzing out of the kitchen into the hallway. Then she pretended that the front door was her dance partner while opening it. I followed her lead out the front door. We must have looked like fools with how over the top we were acting, heading out of our cul-de-sac. I only noticed that we lived in a cul-de-sac because of our playful banter.

I learned during our walk that our cul-de-sac was still in the city but ten miles away from the heart. We must have had a long walk from the Night's Spring Club last night. It's hard to believe that this would have been my home and neighborhood had my mom not died. Did my Aunt Madeline know my mom used to live here? I wonder if I worried them by now. I can't help but wonder about a lot of stuff. Still, I should focus on learning how to hunt for now. Even if things change, like if the council decided I can't live with my family and I can't have an amulet of my own. I'll need to know how to hunt to survive.

We walked for thirty minutes before we saw a group of people walking out of a bar. All of them looked drunk but one. The one who looked sober reminded me of Bruce. I can't stop feeling angry about what likely happened to Sasha. That person seemed to be having their own hunt with one of the drunken companions of the group. If I wasn't a vampire, I'd want to give that person a piece of my mind. Yet I recalled Kalt's conversation with me about what makes a one-night stand. Also, after reading about the taboos that created vampires, what right does a vampire have to judge a human's behavior? At the end of the day, their living energy is our food. Even if I disagree with their behavior, August and I are hunting also.

I thought we would start a conversation with the group, but August keeps walking and points to her amulet discretely. She wants me to feed while walking past the group of drunks. I can't say that I can focus as well while walking. However, I need to try. Just try to focus, I told myself. I tried to picture myself as a bag of water and picture the sound of the drunk conversation as waves moving the water. I pictured the waves moving from the bag edges to the center with compressed energy. It's hard to imagine with my eyes open and aware of my surroundings. Cars were flying on my left side. The drunk group took up most of the sidewalk. We managed to walk around them safely and continue on our way.

August noticed my frustration after we were out of earshot from the drunks.

She said, "Don't worry if you didn't get a lot."

I felt like I barely got any energy from that compared to breakfast. I think I managed to eat a little since I can feel renewed energy. I suppose my focus needs work. I'll need to consider how much energy I could have eaten or missed due to a lack of skill. Once I have the talent to consume energy mastered while moving, I can determine what situations are good to feed on. I must have been looking serious and lost in thought.

August noticed and continued to explain by saying, "Most walk-bye feedings don't offer a lot of energy. It's because the hunt is kept short. Try to think of the amount as the same as picking a single berry from a bush. It's not going to quench hunger. Yet it gets you what you need for the moment. I'm glad that you were willing to try to feed. In situations like that, an amulet is more efficient for collecting energy. With an amulet, we don't need to focus on our energy, and we don't have to worry about missing any free energy. You could treat it as a quick snack if you want to do both simultaneously."

I felt better but a little foolish for trying to feed. At least I can better understand why an amulet is a necessary tool for hunting. Though, I'm sure that even an amulet has its limits. That makes me wonder if there's any situation where a vampire could eat well without an amulet and without drawing attention. I wanted to let August know that I heard what she said despite my mind wanting to wander off with more questions.

"I see. Then a situation like that one isn't bad but not an ideal situation for a large feeding. And an amulet really is an ace for discreet and effective hunting. I wonder what situations would be preferable for a vampire without an amulet of their own. I mean, I can imagine that there have been times vampires hunted without amulets since they're manufactured," I said.

August put her arm around my shoulders as we continued walking.

"There are a few ways. I plan to show you one fruitful way to hunt as you are tonight. That is where we're headed. I want you to understand that learning to hunt is hard for anyone. I don't want you to feel like you need to hunt perfectly. Nor do I want you to get upset if you haven't gotten your fill of energy. We have my amulet to share. You will never go hungry. I have had plenty of years to learn to hunt well for myself. I can take care of myself without needing to rely on the energy in the amulet. Last night was the only time I truly needed to eat from it while trying to find you," she said.

"I have a question about vampire tricks and energy, but I don't feel I understand enough about how the two are related to ask my question. I think it would have taken more than an illusion to find me. Was it a transformation with the amulet's energy that helped you?" I ask, feeling odd.

August gave me a side hug and said, "I'm glad to tell you everything. But for now, we need to worry about one thing at a time. Let's finish our hunting lesson. Then we can discuss our vampire skills and what happened last night."

After that, we didn't talk for the rest of our walk. Occasionally we'd walk by groups of sober and drunk people. August would point to her amulet to tell me I could try feeding. The second time I tried hunting while walking was with a sober group of high school girls. It looked like they were hanging out and eating cheap, greasy food at a gas station. As we passed by, they started laughing at something that happened. The energy I managed to get felt less than the first feeding. I wondered why.

I thought I did a better job focusing on feeding than last time. It might not have anything to do with what I'm doing. Like August told me, I may have to accept and treat the walk-bye as a berry from a berry bush. I should not expect much.

The third time, three drunks were walking down the sidewalk. I did my feeding trick but was startled. While August and I were walking away, two of the three drunks started following us. They were trying to flirt with us and get our attention. August quickly glanced over to me and then fixed her eyes forward. We continue to walk away without a word. I don't know how long our walk was with our creepy drunk company. Eventually, the two drunks got bored of us and left.

August broke the silents and told me, "You did well. Having those two follow us for as long as they did was uncomfortable. It rarely happens. But when it does, pretend they are not there and eat as you can. If in any situation they take it to the point of physically harassing you, do what you would do as a human in that situation. Whatever you feel is expected by cultural norms. However, keep in mind that we're stronger than humans. If you do strike back, keep your power in check."

More moments of silents passed as we kept walking before she said, "Just around this corner is the best park to hunt for a good meal and rest. Again, don't worry if you feel like you can't get a good feeding right away. It takes time to feed around activity and distractions."

When we got to the park, I was amazed at how many people were there. It was particle buzzing with activity. Every park bench was full. People created their own spots to sit and rest. Some groups had blankets, and others had outdoor chairs. Some sat on the park's wall to face a temporary pop-up stage. Performers would go on the stage with instruments and play music. Others went on the stage with small groups to sing songs. I did not know many of the songs. I knew of a few, like the song, The Rabbit King. I guess many of them were original, but it could also be due to my lack of exposure to the arts growing up. I mostly knew songs that my friends would listen to on the radio. I only knew about the song The Rabbit King from Sasha's father's playlist. I felt like I had walked into a dream. I always wanted to visit places like this growing up. The atmosphere is so warm and peaceful. Can I really be in a place like this? I asked myself. I look over to August. She seemed to be taking in her surroundings. Most likely, she was focused on taking in the energy for a meal. I should try to do the same.

As August predicted, it was challenging to focus on eating as it was while walking. Every odd moment when I felt comfortable in my concentration, something would snap me out of my feeding trance. It was mostly due to people applauding the musicians or singers on the stage. Rarely was it a baby crying during a song, a loud sneeze, or a cough. Yet even with all that noise, I felt like I had my fill. When I checked on August, she seemed content and full too. August noticed that I was checking on her.

"This is a great place because this park has a talent night for the community that is free throughout the week. Twice a week, they have family-friendly shows that can get quite lively. Three nights are for a more mature community, and the songs have more creative freedom. Even though fewer people show up on those nights, this park is always packed. Sometimes they have markets here around the holidays," August said with a smile.

She stretches and asks, "Are you ready to go? There is still plenty for us to do before dawn."

I nodded but was unsure.

I almost felt heartbroken leaving the park so early, even though I was full of energy. I wish I could sing there with the other artist. Perhaps one night, I will. As we walked away from the park, I gave August a side hug. She was surprised and paused her step before hugging me back.

"Thank you for taking me to that park, August. You don't know how much it meant to me. I know it was for the lesson, but I've always wanted to see a concert like that. I never could while I was human. At least not without getting into trouble," I said to August.

"We already know that about you, Roxanne," she told me in a sweet tone, "You love music as much as your mother did. It must have felt cruel not being able to be around places like that. And as much as I hate to agree, your aunt and uncle were right not to take you to places where you could sing. Especially if you're indeed your mother's daughter."

I looked at her with confusion.

"I don't understand. I know my mother loved music and theater. From what my aunt told me, she never got far with her music career like many artists. Yet it sounds like you're implying that there was something more to my mother," I said.

August sighs and looks me in the eye. She jesters a seat and rests in a quiet, empty area close to the park.

"You know why we went to the park today, Roxanne?" she said, but it sounded like a question.

I nodded.

"People like us attend for more than music and entertainment," she said, flustered with her words.

She seemed to have difficulty finding the next words she wanted to say. We sat silent until a familiar voice piped in from somewhere.

"My Aunt Aria Rosewell was a normal lady. She loved music and had a unique gift for connecting, magnifying, and intensifying the emotional energy of those who heard her sing. Where many people can sing and sing well, it's different when a song is sung with a heart that can resonate with those who listen. She also had other musical talents that very few people possess. Such as breaking her voice and singing two different songs simultaneously. Many would consider it a useless talent. Her passion for what she loved would bring her to the places where all three often collect. That is why she unknowably ended up learning about our town. If you had embraced music while living with your aunt and uncle, any of the three kinds could've collected from your song's energy until you woke. Right, Princess Red," a familiar voice said.

I looked around for the voice and saw a small streak of white falling from the tree branches. The next thing I knew, Kalt was standing beside our bench wearing a different white suit than the night before.

He was wearing a white formal dress vest. He was also wearing white dress gloves. He had a pale blue bow and bloodstone hiding in his vest pocket. Well, that would be my guess. It wasn't on him like last night, and something was in his vest pocket. Did he finish hunting? I wonder how hard it is to hunt for blood and fill a bloodstone. August stood up and grabbed Kalt's collar like last night.

"What did I say about the nicknames, Kalt?" August asked with a lot of anger in her words.

"Why are you so mad? I got the gender right this time," Kalt replied.

August wouldn't have it, and her grip tightened.

"As much improved as the notion might seem to you. It doesn't address my desire for those nicknames to end. I have a name, and that's enough," she said.

Kalt didn't seem fazed by August's attempt to address his behavior. I wonder if he is getting a kick out of it. I still felt confused and wanted to ask more questions. Like if a vampire could feed on a half-breed whose blood was still sleeping? But I felt this was not the time. They needed time to work this mess between them out. Kalt managed to break out of August's grip and turn his attention to me.

He fixed his collar and said, "Your mother might not have been anyone special to everyday people. However, she was a gem for us. My uncle was very lucky to have been given the honor of being her protector and husband. Many bet you would inherit your mother's gifts, dear cousin Voxy."

August tried to grab Kalt again, but he managed to evade her.

"She has a name too, Kalt," August snapped, "Her name is Roxanne. Not Voxy."

"Honestly, no one here cares about names as much as you," Kalt said in a cold, indifferent tone.

August looked like she'd kill him if she had a chance. I wanted to see if things would work out, but I felt it would only worsen if I let the matter continue.

"Kalt, may I ask what brings you here? I thought you would be working at your club," I asked to change the subject.

"A business owner isn't the same as a manager, cousin. I own the club, but I don't work there. I only need to check in occasionally to ensure it operates legally and effectively. As for why I am here, I am collecting like you and August. When I saw you two leaving the park, I decided to tag along for fun. Also, I wanted to see how you were adjusting to our town," Kalt said in a kinder tone than when he talked to August.

I suppose by collecting, he is talking about hunting. I wonder if he chooses his words carefully if someone from the park happened to walk this way and overhear.

"So, how has your first day in our little town been, cousin?" Kalt asked.

"It's been eventful, Kalt," I said.

Before I could say more, August chimed in. I have to say I am thankful. When Kalt focuses on me, I feel like I'm his prey. It feels like he is waiting to find a weak point to go after. This must be what August had talked about. How Kalt will hold power over others when he discovers their weakness. I find it harder to believe that he loves his family.

"Why are you in our clan's territory and collecting? You're not allowed to collect in another clan's territory," August spat out with frustration.

"I did not say I was collecting in your clan's territory, August. I said I was collecting. I came over to greet you since the line between territories is only a foot away from this side of the park," Kalt explained, sounding annoyed.

"Territories?" I mainly asked to defuse the possible fight they would have if Kalt kept pushing August's buttons.

"Yes, unfortunately, that is a little harder to explain without a map. A short answer is what it sounds like. Each clan has an area that they can wander and call home. There are areas where the edge of one area meets another clan's home area. A foot over there is my clan's home. And the club is also located," he tried to explain, "I can explain it better to you during your visit to the council in a few days, dear Roxanne. There will be a map of our town to help show what's were. If August or the others don't explain it to you sooner."

August seemed ready to end the conversation with Kalt. I think I am too. I don't know why given that I feel like I ate well, but I feel a wave of fatigue. I know that August wanted to teach me a few things before dawn. I am starting to wish that I had slept better.

"I saw that you ate well for your first day in our town," Kalt said, "But the change in time can take its toll on anyone. I could keep you company while August finishes her outing."

August wouldn't have it.

August said, "Roxanne will have difficulty adjusting to the time difference if she doesn't try to stay awake more during our days, Kalt. Besides, I still have one more monument to show my sister before calling it a day."

I try to keep up with their conversation. I wonder if anyone passing by could really understand any of this. Or feel confused like I do? I have some background knowledge of what they're trying to say. I'm sure this would sound more like drunks arguing about weird stuff to each other for an average person. August and Kalt would've looked like they had lost their minds if anyone were watching this. I decide to end the dispute about rest and who will help attend the venture to the last key monument of our town.

"Thank you for your concern and desire to help, Kalt. I am sure I'll have many opportunities to learn from you about this town. However, I'd like to see this last monument with my sister and call it a day. You've been kind enough to notice I am getting tired, and this interesting conversation isn't helping. It was good to see you again, cousin," I said, trying to sound polite.

Although, I really didn't care how it came across.

"I understand, my dear cousin. I will respect your decision on the matter," Kalt said in a way that I couldn't read how he felt, "If you should need me or simply want to talk, then you know where you can go to get ahold of me, Roxanne. The club's doors will be open to you. "

He started walking away.

Then he stopped to say, "O', I almost forgot to mention. You don't need to worry about Bruce working there if you stop by. I let him go. As we discussed last night, Bruce's luck has run out. The girl with the green hair hasn't filed a complaint. Except she was confused when we inquired about Bruce's drunk-induced one-night stand with her. If your sister isn't hell-bent on not using nicknames, I think it might be good for you to check in on her when you are able. Not as her old friend but as a concerned bystander happy to lend an empathetic ear. Also, give my regards to my cousin Julia. She did a good job giving you a new look."

He started to walk away again after that.

August and I did the same. I've no idea where we're heading, but I hope it's close to home. My mind is buzzing with worry for Sasha. I wish I knew what happened, and I could go check on her now. Yet I can't. I know Sasha well enough that she would feel devastated if Bruce lost his job over something like this. She'd feel responsible for what happened to Bruce and not acknowledge that the situation was Bruce's own fault. To her, Bruce was everything. She never would file a complaint or consider herself a victim. She'd only ever give Bruce the benefit of the doubt. I hate that situation. I can't help her, and I doubt I could visit her with how tired I feel. After all, my life is not what it was. I'm not her old friend. We're nothing more than strangers now. My thoughts were disturbed by the sound of August's voice. I didn't ask what I missed. I only looked over at her.

"I know that you want to help Sasha. You two have been friends for years. You need to trust her and let her work this out between them. She will not be happy for some time, but she'll become a happier woman someday, with or without him. For now, you have a lot on your plate. When the time is right, I'll look after you while you reconnect as a stranger to her. Unfortunately, she lives in his territory. I don't think you'll be safe going there alone," August said.

All I could bring myself to do was nod.

"We're close to home. There is a park nearby that is barely visited I want us to go see. We'll work on helping you learn how to control living energy. I think that'll be well worth the trip. After all, I refuse to let Kalt take away your joy," August said, sounding determined.

Children of The Red Wolf

The park barely had any streetlights. It had dense tree coverage, hardly letting any starlight reach us. Yet, I can still see clearly in the darkness. I hadn't noticed that I had left August behind at the park entrance. I would have continued to walk away if she hadn't yelled for me to come back. I turned around, and instead of seeing August, I saw a red furry four-legged beast with glowing yellow eyes and sharp teeth that glistened with the little light present. It wasn't large. I'd say it was about the size of a big dog. It looks too wild to be a pet. It's too big to be a red fox. Could it be a wolf?

What is a wolf-like beast doing in a city park? The beast changed its posture from hostel-looking to calm. It almost looked like a majestic beast. The beast had decided to sit on the sidewalk and close its mouth for me. After a moment of waiting to see what the beast would do, it lowered its head to me.

I thought I heard August saying, 'It's alright, Roxanne, the red wolf is me. You can pet my head if you want.'

After the shock of hearing August's voice, I asked, "Are you really a wolf? Is that really you?"

The wolf looked up at me, panting like a dog and moving its tail, happy to see its family.

'Yes, the wolf is me, Roxanne. This isn't a normal transformation for vampires. It's a unique ability we've inherited from our father. You asked earlier if I needed to transform to find you. I did. I had to switch between a wolf to find your scent and a bat to cover more ground quickly. Switching between forms and becoming human a few times uses a lot of energy. I remember you said you don't know German, but do you happen to know what our family name means, Roxanne?' I heard August's voice ask.

The wolf tilted its head inquisitively to the question.

"No, I am afraid I don't know what our family name means, August. If it's something to do with the transformation, my guess would be red wolf?" I said thoughtfully but concerned.

"That's not a bad guess, Roxanne," I heard dad's voice say from a distance. His shadow showed up before his figure appeared by the entrance gate.

He looked at August's wolf form and said, "I think you demonstrated the effectiveness of our family's transformation well, August. You may turn back now. Let us see Roxanne try the wolf transformation."

The red wolf's figure changed shape into that of a person. To be exact, the person was August, now standing beside our father. I was concerned that she would've been in her birthday suit. Thankfully, she was still in her clothes after her transformation back.

"If I am close in my guess, father, what does the family name mean?" I asked.

He looked at me with his usual loving fatherly air.

He started with, "The name Kurt is Turkish for a wolf. You were right to guess the word wolf. However, the person in our family whose name means red wolf is me. It's not my name originally. I was given the name by an old vampire friend who lived in the country of Turkey many years ago. When I became a true vampire, I couldn't see myself as I once was. My friend gave me a new name for my new life as a vampire."

He took a long deep breath and said, "I'm sorry I haven't taken the time to share my name with you, my Roxanne. It's not easy for the people in this country to say. Consequently, I don't have a habit of telling my name to people. I'll tell you my name, though. My name is Kirmizi Van Kurt. You may continue to call me father if you have difficulty saying my name."

He walked over to stand next to me and asked, "Now do you feel ready to try a wolf transformation?"

I felt a chill run down my spine.

"What if I mess up and get stuck as some mutated thing?" I blurted out.

August smiled and said, "That's why you have father and me here. We can transform you back if you get stuck."

"The process of transforming is simple if you have a solid image of what you what to transform into in mind. You had a chance to see August Wolf form. Do you remember the water bag trick for eating energy? Instead, imagine the wolf shape instead of a bag and fill the shape with water. Remember the waves you see as you collect living energy. Now imagine moving those waves in the opposite direction," dad said in a calming tone.

I took a deep breath. I want to do this at my pace. I'll focus on the image of August when I saw her wolf form. I breathed and imagined the image changing to show a wolf's silhouette filled with water. The waves of repelling water moved from the core to the edges. I started to feel something warm. I felt hair growing in between my fingers and toes. My back was feeling like an invisible force was making an arch. My spine felt stretched and elongated. I feel my nails, and what once were fingertips touch the cement under me. My ears felt like they were moving higher on my head. And my teeth felt sharper. When I felt the change was done, I took my time letting go of the wolf's image and opened my eyes slowly to reality.

"O'! You're so adorable!" I hear August say with squill of delight in her voice.

I felt confused. I feel small. My paws are tiny, and my legs aren't long. I don't think I did it right. What could I have done wrong? Did I spend too much time imagining the wolf that it became some pint-sized furry mess?

"Roxanne language," father said, clearly upset.

What language? I thought that I was thinking to myself. I don't think I said anything. What does he mean?

"This is what I mean. A transformation required many vampire skills to be used all at once. Each skill involves using energy. All these skills remain active until you learn to control and stop their energy flow. The process of controlling or stopping energy flow is called an energy filter. You must develop an awareness of how you use energy to create energy filters. Right now, you have used a transformation with energy, and telekinesis is a skill linked to that transformation. Your telekinesis has no filter to prevent your thoughts from being shared with us. When you learn more about telekinesis as its own separate skill, you can prevent the flow of sharing your thoughts and keep them private in this form. Unless you have something you what to share in this transformation with others," dad said.

August pulled out an old pocket watch and opened it. She sat down and held the pocket watch out for me to see. A mirror was on the opposite side of the clock, and I saw my reflection. I look like a puppy but hairier.

"You're a wolf cub, Roxanne. You did the transformation perfectly. You didn't look like an adult wolf because your blood just woke. Your vampire blood is considered young. So, your transformations will be child-sized for the first few years," August said, trying to assure me that I'd someday be an adult wolf like her.

I smiled weakly back.

Well, this transformation is a bit of a bust if I want to scare a creep away.

"Don't worry, your plenty strong as a vampire. If you need help, we're around and not going to leave you defenseless," dad said while petting my cub wolf coat.

O' that reminds me, dad... a father. You were working with Julia today to prepare for the council meeting. I didn't mean to pull you away if she needed your help. How did that go?

"First change back. I can start to feel the heat of the sun. Which means it will be morning soon, likely in an hour," dad said with concern.

August explained to me how I could transform back into my old self. It was like the wolf and the feeding trick. Before imagining water, I had to have a solid image of what I looked like. Like the wolf, I must move the energy from the inner to the outer frame. Again, I took my time with the process. I felt the change; it was colder with less hair on my person to keep me warm. I felt my fingers grow and my nails get smaller. I felt my legs and arms change and my back recoil with no tail. My nose and ears moved back to their proper place on my face. My teeth change back to molars in the back. I have to say I feel truly thankful that my clothes changed with my body, so I wouldn't be running around in my birthday suit.

I wonder if they heard that last thought.

I asked, "Have you heard any thoughts of mine?"

August piped up and said, "Nope, you are back to you. We might ask Julia to cut your hair again tomorrow. You might've pictured the way you used to look. Your hair is back to a bowl cut, but that's fixable."

I grabbed the hair on my head and pulled a hand full forward to my face. August was right.

"I see. Sorry about that," I said sheepishly.

"Your find Roxanne. I am proud of how quickly you picked up on transformations. Now is it still frightening?" dad asked.

"Your right. It's not that bad. It is scary to think about how easy it is for anyone to hear my thoughts. Not much privacy," I said, "Anyway, father, you need to answer my question about Julia. I changed back now."

He laughed.

"Yes, I did agree to tell you. We finished our conversation about half an hour before we could see August and you heading to the park. So, I came out to meet you both. I didn't want to miss my youngest trying her hand at her first transformation. I'm so glad to be able to see your wolf form. I am proud that the transformation to and from was not a problem for you. As for telekinesis, you'll learn how to control it with practice. That said, I want you to try eating one more time tonight. Transformations do use up a lot of energy. It uses even more when you have no filters to control your other abilities," he said as he walked back to the park entrance. August and I followed him home.

Julia was sitting on the patio swing with a far-off look. She realized we were back when we got close to the front door. I wonder if I looked like this last night when August tried to get my attention to introduce me to them.

"Welcome back, you two. How was your hunt this evening?" Julia asked in her usual chipper voice.

"We went to the best feeding ground in the territory. You know, the one with the freelance musicians playing in the park. Roxanne loved being there," August said.

"It's true. I always wanted to go to places like that, but you know my Aunt Madeline and anything creative," I said with joy and my usual frustration.

"I understand that you feel like you've missed being able to make lots of good memories, Roxanne. I'm glad that you can visit places like that now. To enjoy and eat to your heart's content. Nonetheless, I am thankful that your aunt and uncle did their best to keep you safe," Julia said while standing up to greet us at the door.

"We also did some walk-by feedings. And Dad met us at the park close to home for Roxanne's first transformation lesson," August said, continuing to explain the evening's events too Julia.

Julia looked at me.

"I can see that you managed to change back successfully. I'll give you a haircut tomorrow. To be honest, Roxanne, even Amelia, and August had long hair after their first two months of learning transformations. Amelia has the best transformation story involving hair. I think that because of that experience, she's been reluctant to let me comb her hair nowadays," Julia said.

Julia led me to the living room.

"Let me tell you the story, Roxanne. August heard of it from our mother when she started her transformation training.

Everyone knows the story, and it's a good one," Julia said with a smile.

She plopped herself on a cushion and pointed to the seat I was sitting at this morning.

"Get comfortable while I figure out where the best part to start the story.... Right. When Amelia was seventeen years old, which would technically be a child. It is a normal age for teaching transformations. Therefore, Roxanne, you're still considered an appropriate age by our culture's customs to begin learning illusions and transformations. However, she would look like a five-year-old if she was human. She acted like one, too," Julia said, trying to reflect on how to tell the story and continued.

"The day after her seventeenth birthday, our mother took her to a deserted field where we lived in Germany. The first time she transformed, she managed to transform into a very long-haired fruit bat. Despite our mother's instructions and showing her what the transformation was supposed to look like, Amelia was not interested in learning to control or master her abilities. She loved manipulating the length of her hair. At the end of her lessons, she had miles-long hair. Our mother taught me how to work on taming and styling hair because Amelia's fascinated with long hair. On the first summer night, Amelia made it her personal goal to cover the whole field with a layer of her hair. Now that you've had a chance to experience a transformation, you can understand how we use a lot of energy. Especially when we can't control our energy. Amelia transformed with no one around to watch her for over an hour. She was passed out when we found her at the field we trained at. Half of the field was covered in a long rat's nest of hair. It took all three of us to carry her home. If you want to know why we did not cut her hair off and leave it there, the short answer was we couldn't afford to risk creating suspicion. Even if the field was abandoned at night, any villager who could find their way to the field could raise a voice of concern and get the village worked up. We worked hard that night to get Amelia's energy back and give her a good haircut. We had to be creative in dealing with the long lock of hair left behind. We worked out the tangles, and mother spun the hair into a threat to hide it. When Amelia came too, she was sick for two weeks and angry that we ruined her hard work and the greatest masterpiece. She would never trust my mother or me with her hair for a long time. Our mother ended up in her good books regarding hair trust after August was born," Julia said.

"That sounds like how I've experienced Amelia. Still, I wonder what your mother did to get her to trust her with her hair," I said.

"If I knew that answer, I promise you our sister would never have a day where her hair looks like it has never met a brush. Mother was the only one who knew, and she had never told me anything about her trick," Julia said with a sound of defeat.

"Speaking of which, has Amelia gotten back from Port 72 yet?" our father asked Julia as he walked into the room.

"I'm afraid I've not seen her yet. I hoped she would have gotten back by now," Julia replied.

Father headed out the front door after that. I bet he is going to go looking for Amelia before the sunrises. It's soon, and I'm feeling tired. My blanket and pillow from this morning are in the corner. Since things seem quiet now, it might not be a bad idea to read a book while waiting for Amelia and bedtime. I decided to read a different book than the one I read this morning. This one is on the history of illusions. I notice a short chapter on the vanishing reflection illusion in the table of contents. Julia likely read this book and remembered what was written in the chapter. I flipped to that chapter out of curiosity and skimmed the first paragraph. Yep, this is likely where she got it from. Though the chapter has more information than Julia shared. I started reading the book from the beginning until dad and Amelia returned.

When I finished reading the fifth page of the chapter on aging illusions, I heard the front door slam shut. Amelia marches into the living room without a word and drops a white box with a silver bow on me.

"There, the undesirable mystery package has been delivered," Amelia said, plopping down in a chair next to our father's chair.

Then she looked at me for a moment and said, "What in the world did you do to your hair? I thought that Julia gave you a haircut today."

I honestly couldn't tell if she was serious or poking fun at the fact that I messed up my new look with transformation practice.

"Julia did cut my hair today. However, I messed up the transformation back into a person from a wolf. From what I have been told, it's a typical mistake to make," I said while examining the box.

It doesn't look like it has a letter or any writing on the wrapping paper. How would she know it's meant for me?

"You said this was delivered, but I don't see any writing on this box. How do you know it's meant for me?" I asked.

"Father removed the card that was with it. It was at Port 72 and handed to me by one of our members. Apparently, someone dropped off the gift for you there. From what the man told me, it was there for hours before I showed up," Amelia said, "They also told me your sound stone will be ready to get in two weeks. Think you can manage...."

Amelia froze with a look of concern. While she was talking, I opened the gift. Inside the box was a blue heart-shaped stone amulet on a silver chain. August walked into the room and saw Amelia's face.

"What's wrong?" August asked.

Amelia pointed to the box. August turned to face me and saw the box with the blue heart amulet.

"Where'd you get that?" August asked.

"Amelia said someone from Port 72 gave this to her, and it was addressed to me," I told August, "I am confused. I don't get what those looks are for. It's just a piece of jewelry."

"Oh no, it's not," August replied with horror.

"What's the commotion?" Julia said as she walked into the living room, standing behind August.

"Someone sent Roxanne a courting stone," August answered.

"A what?" I asked.

Did I misunderstand what she said? Julia sat beside me and picked up the amulet from its box.

"It's made with sound stone materials at least. You can feed on this in the meantime," Julia said while examining the stone.

"Do we know who sent this?" Julia asked.

Amelia moved from her seat to sit on my other side.

Amelia answered with, "Father would be the only one who knows. He took the card that was with it. I didn't care to check. From what I can tell, no one from our clan knows Roxanne's blood woke up. It was likely left by someone outside."

All three were looking at it, and no one spoke.

I broke the silents by asking, "I thought sound stones are red. Why is this one blue?"

"Sound stones are clear and can be dyed any color. We normally color them red to show solidarity with bloodstones. However, when it comes to courting a sound vampire, a gift of a blue sound stone is traditionally given," Julia replied.

I tried to take in all the information. What stood out in my mind was that we didn't know who sent it. Nor do we know how to send the thing back. After all, I don't want to accept this person's proposal for a relationship. I likely never meet them. I continued to examine the box for any clue I could find.

"Aren't gifts like these often given in person?" August asked, "After all, you gave yours in person, right, Julia?"

"Yes, I did because I am of age, and the person I courted was also of age. Roxanne is too young for someone to court her properly," Julia said.

"The person who sent it is likely of age. They would have to be in order to have a stone like this made," Amelia said.

That information could help narrow down the list if I knew what the list was. The sender would have to be 2000 years old or older and know my blood woke. If the clan doesn't know, that will make sense. I haven't met anyone outside my family. As I looked at the box and stone again, I felt unsettled.

"Julia, I know that our father married your mother. You all are related to a blood-eating vampire. As much as I hate to say it, I might have a possible idea of who may have sent this. But it depends on a few things. First, could a blood-eating vampire of age order a courting sound stone if the person they're interested in is a sound vampire? If they're of age and bold enough to try this, there is one person I could think would do this. Apart from our family, the only other vampire who knows my blood is awake is...." I said but could not bring myself to finish the thought.

"Father could be confronting Kalt right now if he recognized his hand. Kalt is of age this year like Julia," August said, suppressing her anger.

"That would explain why father took off and told me to head home," Amelia said.

"But even Kalt would know that he can't court Roxanne. It's inappropriate," Julia said.

"Isn't this situation, in general inappropriate," Amelia retorted.

We all agreed it was.

August pulled out her pocket watch and looked at the time.

"It's dawn now. I doubt Father will be able to come home any time soon. He'll likely stay in their family's manner," August told us.

"Will our father be alright?" I asked.

"He'll be fine. I think we will need to go to bed without him. Let's put this gift up in a safe place and try to get some sleep," Julia said like a mother assuring her children.

We went to our rooms and went to bed to call it a day. Amelia's behavior toward me seemed to have softened now. She asked if I wanted to sleep in her room until the evening. I appreciated the gesture but explained that I could still wake at odd hours of the day. I wouldn't want to disturb her rest. She understood, and I returned to my room to sleep. So crazy of a day.

8

Days fly by

The house was quiet when I woke up. I wonder what time it is. It could be close to evening. Even if that's the case, it would've been nice to have had more time to continue my experiment from yesterday. I know where I can get strands of Amelia's hair and mine after yesterday's haircut. I can see if there is a difference in the reactions or appearance after being exposed to sunlight. I got out of bed and went to the living room to see what time it was. When I checked the living room clock, it read 3:40 pm. Okay, I remember where the moon was when we hunted. The sun would follow a similar course. The sun could reach the hair strands best by the kitchen window at this time of day. Perfect! The hair is in the kitchen trashcan. I don't have to go far for what I need.

I left the living room and went to the kitchen. The hair was easy to find. Picking out the hair by length took a little more time. I got long and short strands of hair. Since Amelia has longer hair than mine, I think it's safe to say which belongs to whom. I threaded both hair strands between the window and the curtain. I started counting. After five seconds, I vaguely smelt something burning. When I pulled the hairs back, the longest strands had become shorter. The tip of the strand was smoldering with a pinch of ash. The hair smelled of smoke. Did it burn in five seconds?

My strand of hair looked unchanged, like the first round of experiments. It also didn't smell of smoke. Okay. Well, now I know there is a difference between us despite being related. A person like Amelia wouldn't be able to survive five seconds in sunlight, but I can. When did the hair start to burn? How long will it take for me to do the same? I think I should test mine first since I know what I'm looking for in a reaction. I can rule out five seconds in known sunlight exposure. I'll go for ten. Then I tried fifteen. Then thirty. Then a minute with help from the living room clock. Then three minutes. I kept this up for an hour with the same strand of hair. In this experiment, it took an hour for a slight graying at the tip of the strand. No smell of smoke and no sign of ash.

I better call it a day. Julia, Amelia, and August will be waking up soon. I'll save some strands in my room for tomorrow. I put the few away in my vanity and decided to get dressed. I found some casual clothes in the dresser. I pulled out a light purple top with a pair of blue jeans. After getting dressed, I heard movement outside my door. One of them must be awake. I opened my bedroom door in time to see Julia's bow move downstairs. I wonder if she's going to disappear again. I followed her downstairs and saw she had gone into the kitchen. Again, I followed her into the kitchen.

When I opened the door, Julia sniffed the air and asked, "Where's that burning smell coming from?"

It took Julia a moment to realize I was in the kitchen with her.

"Do you happen to know where that burning smell is coming from?" Julia asked me.

"Yes, it was the result of a little science experiment I was doing over an hour ago," I said with embarrassment.

I could barely tell that Amelia's hair had a burning smell, yet Julia could smell the smoke well after an hour.

"Science experiment? What were you trying to discover from this experiment?" she asked.

I told her about everything. How my body prevented me from opening the curtains yesterday. The light switch led me to a hair experiment to determine how sunlight would affect me. How nothing changed in yesterday's attempt. After learning more about where the moon was to the house and the additional hair after yesterday's haircut, I thought I'd move the experiment to the kitchen. I also told her what I learned from today's experiment and explained the origin of the burnt smell.

"Amelia's strand of hair turned to ash within five seconds of being exposed to sunlight?" Julia asked.

"Yes, but the reaction could have happened sooner. Since my hair's reaction barely changed in an hour," I replied.

Julia stared with a concerned look on her face.

"I don't like this experiment. I fear you will end up getting hurt, and we cannot help you. I know you're doing your best to think through safety concerns. It makes sense that you'd want to know how the sun would affect you and us. Now that you know what you do, can you agree not to continue this experiment anymore?" she asked.

"Sure. I think I know enough now that sunlight is harmful to us. I'll stick to reading when I get up early," I said reassuringly.

"Thank you, Roxanne," she said as she brushed my hair with her hand, "We better clean up the kitchen before the others wake up and smell this, too."

I agreed and was handed the trash bag to take out to the bin while Julia looked for the cleaning supplies. Amelia and August were awake and downstairs when we finished cleaning the kitchen. We went into the living room to talk and eat our breakfast. August shared her amulet with me while Julia and Amelia ate from their own amulets. After I finished eating my share of breakfast, August ate.

"What are we going to do today?" I asked.

Amelia and Julia looked around the room, uneasy.

Julia said, "It's hard to say right now. I don't think it's a good idea for all of us to be outside until dad gets back. Though we'll need to do some hunting."

"If we do hunt," August said, "should we bring 'it' along with us for Roxanne to eat from?"

"Absolutely not!" Amelia said, "She can eat from our amulets as she has been. Her amulet will be ready in a few days, and we'll be fine without using his. The sick man."

"I see both of your points of view. Amelia, I agree that letting her eat from it would make it seem that Roxanne has accepted his proposal to be courted. August, I know this will take some time to resolve. It's best to be prepared for the possible long game. The long game may be his intended plan. That we would have to give Roxanne the stone to feed on," Julia said.

Julia turned to me and asked, "Whatever the choice is, I would rather let Roxanne decide how she wants to be fed. So, what do you think you want to do, Roxanne?"

"I don't know. It depends. I get that there can be traps set by Kalt that we need to avoid. However, I think you know more about this situation than I do. For starters, why can't we all be outside?" I asked.

"Remember how late it was getting when father went out to get me yesterday?" Amelia started to explain, "Father can find us in a moment in our territory and be able to bring us back home in a heartbeat. It'd take Julia, August, and me thirty minutes at least to find whoever was missing. Also, unlike our father, we can lose our sense of time and not know when the sun is about to rise. It is especially easy to lose track of time while hunting."

"You will not be able to continue transformations training, too. We don't know if we can find enough energy close to sunrise," Julia added.

"Are there social areas closer to home?" I asked.

"One café if it's a good night," Julia said, "but if we go there too many days in a row...."

She paused and bit her lower lip.

"There is another problem apart from just hunting and avoiding sunrise. The clan members might notice something is wrong if we visit the same area multiple days. Suppose they get wind that father left his territory without officially informing them I was left in charge during his absence. In that case, they could start thinking they could get away with things that would otherwise be deterred from trying under his watch. Aside from that, many of our clan's social wells are on the edges of our territory. Without becoming a bat, it can take a few hours to get there by foot," August said.

I try to think of what options we have.

"We have sunlight, food, and peoples' plotting to be concerned about for an unknown number of days. Is there anything else we need to consider a problem?" I asked.

"I think that covers most of it. We may have forgotten some minor things, but I think we covered everything major," August replied.

"Hey, correct me if I am wrong with this train of thought. I remember hearing stories about vampires who can control bats to be their extra pair of eyes. Is there some truth to that myth?" I asked.

"Depends. It's not completely off, but it's rare. The problem with having bats as an extra pair of eyes is that they're naturally blind. Any vampire can control almost any animal with a snare illusion. But with a bat, we'll only receive conversations without context," August said.

"It wouldn't take a lot of energy to snare a small animal. Yet if it's like a squirrel, rabbit, rat, etc.. it can take more energy because of their hyper nature. Bugs have many eyes that their vision will make anyone sick while trying to process what they see. Cats and dogs use even more energy because of their reluctant nature due to stubbornness or loyalty," Julia said, trying to further explain.

"The only bats that can be used as eyes aren't normal bats. They've created familiars. Creation abilities are skills beyond illusion and transformation that rarely any vampires possess. The technical name we refer to this ability is called manifestation. It makes something that doesn't exist able to exist, like a knife appearing out of thin air. However, manifested creatures don't have souls. They're puppets that are connected and controlled by their handler. It's even rarer to control a created familiar to look, behave, and sound like the real thing," August said.

"If you want to know if anyone in our family can make and control one, the answer is no," Amelia said bluntly.

"Okay, I think I'd like to give a proposal for you all to judge," I said, "Since the clan members don't know me, nor do they know that my blood is awake yet. Could I go to the café nearby to feed for however long this takes? The clan could only guess I am related to you all. However, if it was just me showing up regularly, I don't think it would carry the same significance as if it were with one of you three. Also, if I happen to lose track of time, you'd know where to look for me because it's close to the house."

"It's not bad. If we agree to your plan, let's keep it to every other day you can go feed at the café. If they do catch on, it will take longer for them to ensure our father isn't around. If we go with this plan, we request that you bring our sound stones, too. It would limit our need to leave the house beyond my regular duty by patrolling our territory. Another reason is in case of an emergency where you need to use more energy, like a threatening situation. We also don't need to worry about going out to fill our stones as much if it's during a single outing," replied August.

"Then, if it's all right with you, may we use this plan?" I asked.

They nodded in approval.

"I think I'll also bring that stone, too," I said.

"Why?!" Amelia blurted out, "The man's sick!"

"In case this does take long. Or if the clan finds out sooner than expected that our father isn't back. I think having extra food around the house will be helpful. No one has to eat from it. It's there as a just in case," I said to reassure Amelia.

Amelia looked at me with sad puppy dog eyes.

"Just don't need to use it ever. I don't want you to get hurt by him. Never ever," she pleaded.

"I won't," I said.

I am feeling curious about which one of us is really the older sister here. It really does not matter. I am glad to be able to have a better relationship with her.

"In the meantime, we can pass our time with simple activities around the house while we're not hunting," Julia said.

They explained where the café was and what streets to take to get there quickly. We decided the best time of day for me to go to the café was early evening. I take turns eating some from each of their stones every other day. With that being the case, they decided to collect energy close to home with one person walking around in the evening on the days I did not go to the café. Julia and Amelia will borrow August's pocket watch when it becomes their turn. Since we had plenty of energy, for now, we decided to wait until tomorrow for me to start going to the café. August would be the first to hunt with all our sound stones during her evening patrol.

That evening came and went before we knew it. So did the next day and the day after that. I had gone to the café twice now, and things seemed okay considering dad's not back. The first time I when to the café, Julia gave me her own courting stone to fill with energy. However, she told me not to let the others know she had it. Like my stone, it would only be used in case food became scarce. She didn't leave much room in that conversation for me to ask her any questions about her courting stone. It might be for the best. Julia can be a little scary when she isn't caring and sweet.

Our days have been quiet after that. I finished reading the book on illusions, one on herbs, and two books about different accounts of vampire history from dad's bookshelf. Another two days passed, and I went to the café again. I see a small group of men who look to be in their late fifty's talking in whispers on the other side of the building. I can't help but notice that none of them have ordered anything to drink when most customers have ordered something. They glance in my direction from time to time.

I can't say I fully understand what they're saying, but they likely have noticed me. It could be because of my striking resemblance to my sisters. One of the men in their group may have noticed that I've been showing up regularly. After all, I've made a mental note of who I see around me each day I visit the café. One of the men in the group has been here twice out of the three times. I tried to stay as long as possible to collect our needed energy. I try not to pay much attention to them, but ignoring their presents is getting harder. I think I better be going. I'm sure my sisters will understand why I couldn't get enough energy today. As I headed out of the café, I felt that one of the men in the group was following me. What should I do? I can't lead him to my house. They will know I am their sister if they're a clan member. They'll know that something is wrong. Even if they are not a clan member, I can't let some creep follow me home. Now, what should I do about this?

I could beat him in a fight if he is human. There is a good chance he'd win in a fight if he is a vampire. I could try to lose him by trying that vampire trick. The only problem is that I never had time to practice. Guess it's better late than never. I imagine a bubble around me while I walk and turn to a nearby alley. Before he could catch up, I used an invisibility illusion with that bubble image. When the man turned into the alley, he looked around, confused. This probably worked because he was a human. Or he is a vampire that can't sense the living energy around the invisibility trick. This was perhaps not the wisest choice I could've made, but it seems to be working. The man took a moment to try to find me. He was careful in his search. He likely guessed that I couldn't have gotten far. After searching, the man left the alley and started walking back to the street, looking angry.

I waited a moment before bringing my illusion down. I thought I felt another person present, but I couldn't tell who. After a few minutes of observing, nothing seemed to move. I decided it was my anxiety over what had happened. I took a breath and started bringing down my illusion.

Then a voice was in my ear that sounded like dad saying, 'Good job keeping safe, my dear Roxanne. I'm glad you've been learning much in my absence.'

I looked around to see if I could find him. He would have to be close to see me use an illusion. He came down to greet me in the form of a red fruit bat. The next thing I knew, he changed back to his usual self. I was so happy to see him that I gave him a hug.

"How are your sisters?" dad asked, hugging me back.

"They're good, but we've all been worried without you," I said, holding back tears.

"I'm sorry for being gone so long out of the blue like that, but I had something important that required my attention," he said calmly.

When I had a chance to talk between breaths of tears, I said, "We found out what was in the white box. We know that you had read the letter...."

"Kalt sent you a courting stone. I could tell from the letter. He planned a lot. When you turned the legal age for an adult in the human culture, he tried to be the first dependable person in your new life. He hoped you'd be inclined to accept his offer if he got off on the right foot with you. He had every intention to use human laws to justify his desire. That is why we couldn't find you on the night of your eighteenth birthday. He managed to bribe some of our clan members to give a false schedule of where you would be that evening. He convinced Bruce to invite you and your friends to the club on your eighteenth birthday. He wanted to build a relationship with you before your blood woke," he said angrily as we walked home, "As for the gift, you can use it. At least until your amulet is ready. You haven't accepted his offer as long as you don't wear it. Only those who wear a courting stone are in an agreed relationship."

"Don't I need to give it back to him? It's not like I will accept his offer," I asked, unsure.

"For our country's legal system till the late 1990s, it was customary to give engagement rings back to the person who offered. Since the 2000s, if it was given to you as a gift, that gift belongs to you. You don't have to give it back to Kalt," he said, still with anger, "We can at least be thankful that his mother is on our side in this mess. She has her own problems. Although when it comes to her son, she'll not let him make a disgrace of himself."

I feel the situation was a little personal for my father. I wanted to say something to help, but I couldn't think of anything. Dad was angry and upset with good reason. All I could offer was my silents and a feeling of appreciation that my family would go out of their way to help me.

I thought about the sound amulets in my pocket and felt like checking them. There was Julia's rose, Amelia's four-point star, August's shark tooth, and the blue heart was with them. I've never used it and am afraid of what it could've cost me if we had no choice but to eat from it. My father looked over at the amulets I was holding in my hand.

"Even Amelia's amulet. Your sisters put a lot of trust in you these last few days. I see what you've been up to while I was away now. It's not a bad plan considering things, but I don't think it will work in the future. Hopefully, we'll have no need for plans like that ever again. I am truly proud of all four of you," he said.

We walk to our house, and my sisters burst through the door to greet our father. He comforted each of them. I watched with a smile and reflected on how things got to this point. If I told myself on the first day that Amelia is a wonderful protective sister like the other two. She advocates for me as if her life is on the line with the greatest passion. I wouldn't have believed a word of it. If I also told myself what Kalt had done to us these past six days, I would have trusted myself even less. I did trust him when we met. As much as I hate to admit it. Tomorrow I will have to present myself before the council. Even if they try to tear me apart from my family. I know my family will stand beside me, trust me, and go to great lengths to protect me from things I still don't know are against me in this new world. They will love me and encourage me to learn even when it becomes uncomfortable for them. I trust these people to stay by my side no matter what the future holds for me.

After Amelia finished hugging our father. She embraces me and welcomes me home. I give back the amulets to my sisters and put the blue sound stone back in my pocket. When we were in the house, dad shared the whole story of what had happened at the mansion of the Van Schlagers and why it took so long to resolve the issue.

Dad starts by explaining his history with Kalt's mother to help me understand. Apparently, she had a thing for dad. After her sister, dad's first wife, died from the bubonic plague during the Middle Ages, she felt snubbed. Apparently, she divorced her husband privately during that time. She told the council that he also died due to the plague, and she wished to be with our father. Father turned down her proposal. Many members were informed of seeing her old husband around their village. They also had proof he was alive. Kalt hasn't had a father in his life since.

With this history explained, dad started describing how he went to confront Kalt with the letter in hand. Kalt's mother was, at first, his protector and demanded that our father leave. He was able to stay after my father gave her the letter from the box. She then became a moderator between her son and father. She gave both sides time to explain. It took time for Kalt to be forthcoming to his mother and uncle, explaining how his actions were just. After hearing things straight from the bat's mouth, his mother finally agreed to correct her son's behavior. She assured my father that an intimate relationship with me wouldn't be permitted. In addition, the sound stone will be a token of compensation for the damage. I can use or not use it as I see fit. After the matter was settled, our father went to find the clan members who gave the false information and disciplined them for their actions against the family.

"I'm glad he will be leaving Roxanne alone. She can do a lot better than him," Amelia said.

"Hey Julia, do you think you'll be ready for the council? I can imagine this hasn't been helpful with everything going on," August asked.

Julia smiled.

"I might make many mistakes in my life, and I still have many more to look forward to. Except presenting my proposal for marriage to the person I truly love and who I know loves me isn't one of them. This mess only helped remind me why being honest about how I feel when it comes to love is not to be treated lightly. I am sorry I couldn't properly introduce you to them sooner, Roxanne. I've known them since we were kids. They often went with me when I was assigned to help watch over you. They knew who you were then and loved you as much as I do. I know you'll love them too when you meet them at the council. They were the ones who inspired August to come out as female after they came out as non-binary before the council. What that makes me, I don't know. I know that I love them more than words can say," Julia said fondly, remembering her love.

Father nodded and said, "They're a child of a family similar to ours. The family was permitted to have many children. They are the third born, like August. Their oldest brother is their clan's future council member. Once the marriage proposal gets approved, they'll be allowed to stay with us if they wish."

"I am confused about why they could not visit us sooner. But I am glad I will be able to meet them soon," I said happily.

Since my sleeping schedule had gotten better during these last six days, I spent the last two dawns in Amelia's room since she wanted to keep me safe. Even though we can rest well knowing the event is finally over, I still wanted to take some time to bond with her. I also feel safe having my sister nearby. Much of what I guessed about her is correct in that she is a very childlike, reactive, and passionate person. I learn during these days that she is very creative and likes to make and build things. Not for science experiments but to see if she can do something never done before. She is surprisingly nimble in handy work, especially for fine detail. I learned that the vanity in my room was one of her handy works. She told me that she was distraught that I was not as happy to meet them as they were to meet me when I arrived home on my first day of being a vampire. She thought I considered myself too good to be one of their sisters. I apologized for seeming to unintentionally give that impression and for being quick to judge her.

The dawn came, and we slept well. The evening came and our time to meet the council was at hand.

9

The Council

I hear Amelia stirring and becoming restless. I don't feel like getting up yet. I know Amelia will take it upon herself to make sure staying asleep in the evening will be difficult, if not impossible. The night before, she used a tuba to wake me up. August started banging on the wall to get her to stop, but it only added to my discomfort with two siblings making loud sounds.

I feel my skin crawling from fear. Even though we have dad, I still dread the thought that I'll have to meet the council today. Despite how I feel, it's only a day, and I'm not going alone. I can't imagine Kalt will be in a good mood, considering that the unfortunate situation had not gone in his favor over the past few days. However, Kalt will be there with his mother. I better get ready to go, even if it makes me sick to think about it. I wake to see Amelia opening the tuba's case.

"Don't! I'm up! I'm up!" I say to Amelia.

"O' good, I don't want you to be late. It's an important day for you and Julia," Amelia said, sounding like a mischievous child.

"Yeah, I know. What will you do today while we're at the council?" I asked in a sleepy voice, "Now that Dad's back, you could probably go where you want in our territory."

Amelia looked lost in thought. I doubt she had thought about what she'd do with us not around.

To my surprise, Amelia said, "I have to pay a visit to our hotel to check on a few case reports of misconduct by our clan members."

"We have a hotel!?" I asked.

"Well, each clan member has a job, and the clan leaders are business owners. Even though Julia and August tend to do more in this line of work, I pick up the slack when operations and misconduct cases become too much for them. With dad being absent, we had to put a fair bit on hold. The hotel is our economic gem. When Julia gets married, I think you'll have to learn how to do this work too," Amelia said.

"I'm sorry I didn't realize how you have an important role, too. Your role is one of the most important ones. You help enable them to do their best. I had no idea how much our family does outside politics," I explained to Amelia.

"It's all politics. However, we can still find ways to be ourselves and have fun," Amelia said.

What I would expect from my child-like, wild, and rebellious older sister Amelia.

"You better go to your room and get dressed. I need to do the same here. Don't forget to eat before you go. It'll be less fun if you're sick at the council meeting," she said while digging through her closet for clothes.

I leave, not wanting to be attacked by Amelia's amazing flying clothes squad. I head to my room. What should I wear for a day like today? As much as I don't care for formal attire, I should try to look respectable for my family. In the past, if I had something important, my Aunt Madeline would go out of her way to buy me new clothes for the occasion. Most of those occasions were academic award ceremonies and only happened four times in my life. The outfits were often boring solid dresses with a bow, plan skin tone stockings, and dress shoes. I know there are some dresses and other formal clothes in the closet. Let's see what we have. I surveyed the closet closely for something I would like to wear and would be acceptable. Not a cocktail dress. O', what about this? What is this bright red thing? It's an attractive red dress with red threadwork of roses etched into it. The sleeves are short, the fabric loose, and it has an airy look.

At first, I thought it was a robe. I'm glad I checked. I would've missed this. However, would the red clash with my hair? Only one way to know. I put on the dress. It fits well, and it's comfy compared to most formal clothes. I hope it doesn't clash with my hair. I must check. The vanity mirror isn't perfect for a whole look, but it's enough for this task. I sat on the vanity chair with my back straight to get a good look. I see dad standing beside the door frame as I check my reflection.

He was straining out his clothes, looking lost in thought. He was wearing a black dress shirt and dark gray dress pants. His sound stone is hanging from his gray bow tie.

"Does this dress work? I don't know what would work," I said, trying to get his attention.

He walked up to the vanity and said, "As long as you feel comfortable and are happy with the lady in the mirror, it will be perfect. It'll show them the best version of you and who you are."

"True, but I don't what to...."I started, but dad cut me off, seeming to know what I'd say.

"Julia can shine her own way. She has for many years now. My dear child, you can never truly take any value away from another person's shine. My beautiful young lady, be yourself and shine. Encourage others to shine their own way who you meet," he said, smiling at me.

"Too much red?" I asked.

"Really? You're asking that from a man whose name is literally red?" he teased, "Everyone would know you're my child. There will be no room for dispute."

We laughed.

"Look at these two fancy people," Julia said.

"I think I have a hat that would look great with Roxanne's dress. If you want to give it a look?" Julia offered.

Julia was wearing her long hair up in a very detailed braided bun. Strands had little white pearls embedded in the design. She was wearing a white dress with printed wildflowers. A bluebird-looking amulet was around her neck. I remembered seeing it the first time I went to the café with all the sound stones. It was Julia's courting stone that she received. Even though she was the one who gave a courting stone.

"I thought you said you gave a courting stone to your partner?" I said, forgetting that Julia warned me not to say anything about having one of her own.

"Yes, I did. When August was looking for me to prepare you for your first hunt, they asked me to meet them. They went out of their way to get me my own, so we can truly be equal in this relationship," Julia said unapologetically for keeping it a secret.

Thankfully she was not angry that I pointed the glaring question out now.

"It's perfect for you. You look amazing," I said.

"Thank you," Julia said.

"I have to agree. All my daughters are beautiful," dad said.

"So, that's what you did on that morning!? After how many times I asked you where you were, you went to see Cronos!" August's voice boomed from the room next door.

"I know you would've pestered me for details. I have my rights," Julia said, raising her voice to match August.

"No! I would've asked for details about what you two did after you excepted their sound stone," August protested, "Knowing Cronos, it would've been quite the tale!"

Julia rolled her eyes and looked at me.

"You'll understand when you meet them. I promise. Cronos has an air about them but is a sweet levelheaded person," Julia said, trying to help me understand.

"I can't wait to meet them," I said.

I start to feel like today could be more interesting than intimidating with this new person in our lives.

After that, it didn't take long for us to finish getting ready for the day. Julia found a black velvet hat with a black rose on the side to go with my red dress. My black boots helped pull the outfit together. We ate from our sound stones. I felt uncomfortable eating from my sound stone, still afraid that doing so would bind me to Kalt's desires. Still, it had energy, and I didn't want to burden the others. I just need to eat discretely while we're out today. I don't wish Kalt to see me use his courting stone. After the four of us went out and said our farewell to Amelia, we headed down the same road August took me to go on my first hunt. Apparently, we'll not be home till tomorrow evening. As we passed the park, I noticed that we were passing the area that borders the point Kalt said was his family's territory. I feel my body tense up. I keep close to my family.

'It will be alright, Roxanne. Many people will be there, and they have more power than Kalt. He will not hurt you. I'll keep you safe,' father said through telekinesis.

I tried to relax and remember that I'm not going alone.

After some time, we found a large gathering of people standing and working their way into a mansion that had a gothic vibe. I'd expect a place like this to be a vampire's home. I would have loved the architectural details. What is holding me back is knowing that it's likely Kalt's home and where father had been these last few days.

"I am surprised the council would meet here," I said.

"When the idea of the council was first created, there weren't a lot of places for us. We'd have to meet in members' homes to have our meeting. We've kept this practice to remember the need for community and hospitality. With how long some meetings in the past were, traveling back and forth between homes was always a pain. The host must ensure that there is room for guests when it's their turn to host," August said quietly.

"O' my, O' my!" We heard a person cry from a distance.

"A beautiful gem has finally awakened!" Someone in the crowd sang with delight.

If I were to describe the person coming our way, I would say they looked like what I would expect from a particular character from a fiction novel. The book was about a traveling home if I recall. I think I read it in middle school. Sadly, the name of the book is lost on me. This person was wearing an elegant black long flowing sleeved dress suit. It had gold thread work of bold shapes of squares on the sleeves and triangles along the collar. Along the collar was an additional detail of some red thread work of a poppy flower in the triangles. Their sleeves also had lacework. Their hair was wavy of an auburn brown lock tied up in a blue bow. They had a blue sound stone that matched the one Julia had. This must be Cronos.

"Hello, little one. The pleasure is all mine. I am beyond glad to finally meet you, little Roxanne," Cronos said sweetly, offering a hug I accepted.

"I know you don't know me. I'm your sister's special person," Cronos said, introducing themselves, "My name is Cronos Sturm. I'm a ton of fun kind of person. So, if you want a good time or a pick me up, you know who to call when you're feeling down."

"I wish I could remember the book's name, but you remind me of a character I read in a fiction book," I said.

"I bet I know the book you're talking about, and that person is my inspiration. I love their free spirit and being a hundred percent honest to who they are," Cronos gushed with delight and said, "We'll get along well, little Roxanne. I can tell by your good taste. If you ever need me, I'll be happy to help lend a hand or an ear as needed."

Cronos then turned his attention to Julia and flirted up a storm with her. Unlike the fictional character, I can see that Cronos only has eyes for Julia in how they interact.

'What do you think of them?' August asked with telekinesis.

"I like them. They're a perfect couple," I whispered back to August.

"We better get ourselves settled in our rooms and checked in. Would you like to come in with us, Cronos?" father asked.

"Thank you for the honor, sir. Sadly I better go in with my family. I'll see you all later when we have free time," Cronos responded.

They gave Julia a kiss on the cheek before leaving and bowed to the rest of us before heading back into the crowd. We made our way into the building, and father lets a staff member know of our arrival. They handed my father the keys, and we made our way to our rooms. Father started handing us the keys when we got to the floor but stopped when he saw something odd. One of the rooms wasn't next to the others. It was on a different floor. Father glared and asked for the keys. He told us to wait while he sorted out the matter. He handed it back downstairs. I think it's safe to guess what might have happened, but we say nothing. After all, our father would take care of the issue before it became a problem. Kalt was either trying his hand again or conveniently forgot this arrangement.

'How dumb does he think we are?' August said telepathically.

'He is a persistent individual,' Julia replied telepathically.

I kind of wish I could use telepathy as well as they could. They must be using a group communication style.

'He isn't even trying to hide it anymore, though,' August thought, 'Is he becoming unhinged because father told him no?'

'I think it's too soon to say anything now. It could've been an oversight. After all, the matter was settled yesterday,' Julia thought.

Julia reminded August that the room arrangements take months of planning in advance.

'Worst case, Roxanne rooms with one of us. That isn't a bad thing given what we've been through,' Julia thought reassuringly to August and me.

'I still can't believe that. Does he really think our father would be fine with that arrangement?' August thought hotly.

'He was overconfident if not ... well, it's in the past now,' Julia thought, trying to end the conversation.

As we waited for our father to return, we saw a few people come and go from their rooms. One lady in a black dress and silver strapped high heels noticed us on their way to their room and stopped to have a conversation. Her hair was short dirty blond, and coerce-looking with no shape. It made her look mousey and mild.

"I suppose you must be Lord Van Kurt's youngest child," The lady said, seeming unsure how to start a conversation with me.

"Yes, my name is Roxanne. And you are?" I asked, trying to help ease the tension.

"Sorry for not introducing myself sooner," she said, sounding friendly with little confidence behind her words, "Everyone here calls me Lady D. Cargy. It's always a pleasure for me to meet the youth of all types. Sadly, I could never have a child of my own. It is how life sometimes works. Some are blessed with gifts to flourish, and others aren't so blessed. What I can say is be thankful for what life you have."

"That is a wonderful piece of advice, Lady Cargy. I hope this last year has blessed you and your clan." father said, returning to us.

" I hope the same for you and your clan Lord Van Kurt. I best be getting ready. It's almost time to gather, and I am sure you all are in the same boat," Lady Cargy said, making her way to her room.

Even though she seemed unsure how to engage, something about her seemed off to me. Since she mentioned that she couldn't have children, I wonder if she was one of the infected. Even though it could still be possible for any person to have fertility problems. I suppose she could still belong to any type. Her fearful posture towards dad and me. I have a hard time seeing her as a clan leader since she sees a child of another clan leader as being higher standing than her. She acts as if she is lower than us. From what August told me, half-breeds tend to be socially lower than most vampires. It could just be her personal style when talking with others, but something still feels off to me.

"Well, Roxanne, I know your sisters would be happy to let you stay with them. Yet I will ask that you stay in my room tonight," father said, "We couldn't find a new room close to ours. I would feel better knowing where you are while we're here. Also, I feel like I've missed too many days being away from you. I want to spend time with you and help you learn more about our world."

I nod, understanding where he is coming from.

However, I would've felt better sharing a room with my sisters. If Amelia had been here, I bet she would have requested that I share her room. Julia would want the free time to be with Cronos. August likely has good acquaintances from the other clans too. I don't know a soul apart from Kalt. Staying by my father's side makes sense.

"Thank you, my child. Hopefully, the next time you need to attend, you'll have more acquaintances and feel safer," father said.

We put our belongings away in our rooms. The room had a similar feel to some of the antique furniture we had at our home, but the space felt darker and colder. Father assured me the room would feel warmer when we slept in our wolf forms.

"I thought transformations use a lot of energy," I said.

"Yes. However, the energy flow will reduce once you've been in the same form for over thirty minutes, and your body knows you'll not change back any time soon. Same as your human form. Only being in a constant state of change uses more energy with transformations," he says.

"I still don't know how to control my telekinesis skill yet," I informed him.

"It's alright. I'll have time to teach you before we go to sleep," he said with a smile.

We met August and Julia in the hallway when dad was ready to go. Together we attended the gathering in the great hall where the council was held. The great room was filled in no time. After finding our places to reside among the council leaders and their families, I watched those who arrived after us find their places. Some people had to stand due to limited seating. I don't know, but I guess many here are present for the census. Others like Julia could be here offering a request that would affect the population of vampires. I wonder if some might be here for other reasons, but I couldn't guess why. I don't doubt I will learn before the end of the day.

I saw Cronos and their family to our left. Lady D. Cargy is on the opposite side of the room from where father and August are sitting. The seat beside her was empty, yet most were filled. I saw Kalt a few seats away from where father sat. A woman who looked like she could be in her mid-fifties sat beside Kalt. It looked like the years were not kind to her. She looked years older than my father. Her hair was getting grayed with some strands of what was likely her original hair color of black. Her eyes were starting to look sunk in. Her mouth was tight and looked like a perpetual scowl. I almost felt sorry for her.

There were so many people in the room I didn't know, but I had a funny feeling like I had met some at some point in time. Perhaps it's hopeful wishing to want someone in this space to know me or feel like I am known. After all, many people here likely know each other. Being the only one in the room who doesn't know much feels uncomfortable. Before my thoughts of loneliness could settle in, a woman in a long black robe walked to the center of the room. She had a gavel in hand and stood at an intentionally placed podium. The buzz of conversation was stilled.

The woman said, "First, I would like to thank our guests and observers for taking the time to witness the precession of order set forth by the council and its meetings. I hope that the transparency of our work for you can help clarify any confusion regarding the laws we set for our people. Recently many have voiced concern about why we pass the current laws regarding our society. The balance of our population and our relationship to the natural world will be an educational experience. We encourage your thoughtful feedback to ensure that our work is the best work it can be for our councils' territories. With representation fair that it can be for all vampires' dignity and meet the reality of our natural world's times."

After her introduction, the clan leaders and their future predecessors were introduced. Then the conversation begins with business. Each clan reported the number of those who died since the last meeting. Some guests of each clan presented to the council the death certificate and acknowledged their relatives' or friends' death since the last meeting. A quick lesson on where the numbers for the populations were last year and how it relates to the current human census was provided. The lady in the judge's robe reminded us that the human population has been shrinking.

"We must be mindful that our population must also shrink to ensure food does not become a concern or scarcity in our daily lives," she said.

The clan leaders reported on who'd been given permission to give birth in their clan since the last meeting. The newly infected were presented first. It was due to their population experiencing the most frequent change among the three types. For them, the perception of a family differed from the other two clans since they couldn't have their own children. They had to receive permission to infect a new person to become a family member. After the infected, those whose blood woke since the last meeting would be reported and presented to the council. At first, no one stood. I didn't know what I should do. Was I supposed to introduce myself to the council and say my blood woke? Then my father stood from his seat and spoke to the council.

"It has been eighteen years since the approval of the birth of a new clan leader child for the sound vampires. A child of a past approval has woken. I am honored to present my youngest, Roxanne Van Kurt. Her blood has woken this year," father said, sounding professional.

August discreetly gestured for me to stand. So, I stood.

"The numbers of the children of clan leaders are off-balance," a man in the back of the room said.

"Even if it was approved eighteen years ago, it doesn't align with today's population change. Lady D. Cargy has refused to infect a successor, and your clan has one more than needed. It might look balanced on paper, but it's not," the man finished saying in a huff.

The woman in the judge's robe thanked the man for the observation. She asked for space for the rest of the blood woken to be presented during the time. I sat when I saw dad sit. Not wanting to stand longer than I had to. I need to admit I felt attacked just for standing. After none was presented apart from me. The lady in the robe reminded them that it is with hope and uncertainty about what the future brings to the human population when a child is planned. A list of children whose blood is still waiting to wake up was reviewed. This was done to see if a correction to the numbers would come soon. Or if they needed to be addressed now. None of the blood-eating leaders have a child whose blood is still sleeping. The child that year to keep balance was born full-blooded to a clan leader called Drakmon. The child died after two years of life due to health complications. In the same year, an infected leader was also killed. It was due to gun violence among the humans of their territory. Then those who had or were in the process of giving birth to children were presented. Those just born presented birth certificates and showed the newborn. Pregnant women offered proof of growth they had in their development process. In the end, the numbers looked even on paper before my blood woke.

In conclusion, the lady in the robe said, "To correct the imbalance, we'll permit two of the blood clan's leaders to have a child. Two infected leaders and Lady Cargy must find and turn potential successors. And one sound clan leader may have a child. While we're on the topic, let us move to the request process for marriage and children during this time."

As the proceedings continued, my mind couldn't help but question the math. Does it make sense for each type of clan leader to have an option for having one more child? Maybe it was to help calm tensions. I don't know. I'm not going to be fixated on it. Many individuals presented themselves requesting marriage. The tension was thick. Many requests for proposals for either type got turned down. Those permitted this time around were turned down multiple times in the past. Many felt they had more right to marriage or children than the youth.

When it was Julia's turn, she presented her proposal to marry Cronos. It was a case beyond the others. She explained why she feels that her relationship with Cronos has lasted long. How they had already experienced change and challenges that many couples wouldn't imagen facing a lot over the years despite being young. Due to their relationship's adaptable and respectful nature, she presented as one assured that she would have the council's permission to move forward in marriage. The council had a hard time finding anything lacking that would see a reason for why they couldn't be married. Julia and my new in-law were given approval with the expectation that they'd wait to have children. I can't say how much was our father's help and how much was her own hard work. I am happy for her.

Before the proposals came to an end, Kalt stood up to speak.

"That's right," the lady in the black rode said, seemingly embarrassed, "It is listed that you are of age. I must apologize, Lord Kalt. But I've been informed that you haven't courted anyone. Do you have a proposal to present to us?"

I see Kalt's mother's face turn white. Then gradually, a light red appears on her complexion. Apparently, Kalt was going against her. He wouldn't do something stupid. Would he? He saw what other people went through. Many got turned down more than they were given approval. He must be mad that my father got the best of him, or he feels he could win over the council's approval like Julia had. Julia's case isn't his case, though. He must understand that, right? Kalt opens his mouth, and my ears go deaf. No, he did not. I refuse! I don't want to get married!

To be continued in Shadows Sing vol.2

Bio about the Author:

Hello everyone. First, thank you for taking the time to read this book. It is my first published work, and I am excited to share more of this mysterious world with you. My name is Alyson Wilson. I may not be the type of person you expect to write this type of story. I am a military child and have lived in eleven different places in the U.S. and once overseas in Germany. I have a B.A. in Business Management. I studied business to learn how to protect my stories. However, I have been scared to write a single story until now. My fear of writing is due to my dyslexia. I am afraid that my lack of an ability to write would get in the way of my stories opportunity to shine. While trying to figure out what to do with my life, I did a year of volunteer work to help a rural community in Chinook, Montana. I know that when it comes to religion, there is a history of pain. I got my M.Div. at Pittsburgh Theological Seminary. I did a year of residency work at the V.A. hospital in Pittsburgh before and during Covid. During that time, I have been challenged to see my disability as a gift and what it means for me to live a life authentic to what I believe, not only in my faith tradition but in myself. I have been encouraged by them to live life authentically, and this book series including even more stories to come is a part of that authentic life. If you would like to read side-stories for Shadows Sing, please visit https://shadowssingsidestories.blogspot.com . For more information about the next books please consider fallowing the author's page on Facebook, Twitter @alysonmwilson2u, and my attempt at drawling these characters on instagram alyson.m.wilson.165 . Thank you all for your support, lovely gems.